White Lilacs

Carolyn Meyer

White Lilacs

Gulliver Books
Harcourt Brace & Company
San Diego   New York   London

Requests for permission to make copies of any part of
the work should be mailed to: Permissions Department,
Harcourt Brace & Company, 6277 Sea Harbor Drive,
Orlando, Florida 32887-6777.

Gulliver Books is a registered trademark
of Harcourt Brace & Company.

Library of Congress Cataloging-in-Publication Data
Meyer, Carolyn.
White lilacs/Carolyn Meyer. — 1st ed.
p.   cm.
"Gulliver Books."
Summary: In 1921 in Dillon, Texas, twelve-year-old
Rose Lee sees trouble threatening her black community
when the whites decide to take the land there for
a park and forcibly relocate the black families to
an ugly stretch of territory outside the town.
ISBN 0-15-200641-9   ISBN 0-15-295876-2 (pb)
[1. Race relations — Fiction.   2. Afro-Americans — Fiction.
3. Texas — Fiction.]   I. Title.
PZ7.M5685Wh   1993
[Fic] — dc20   92-30503

Designed by Camilla Filancia
Map by Eric Hanson
Printed in Hong Kong
C E G F D
E G I H F (pb)

FOR ROSALIND

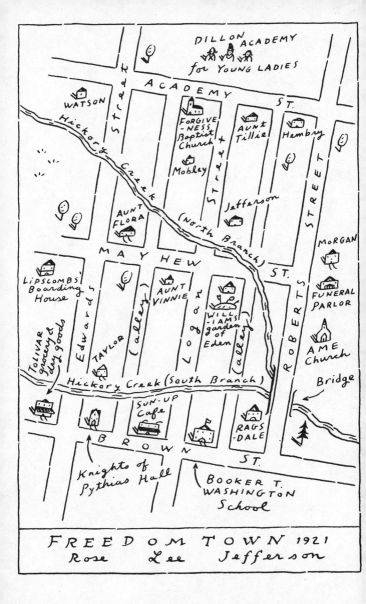

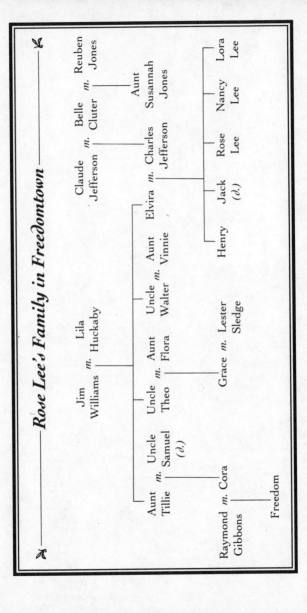

Rose Lee's Family in Freedomtown

Claude — *m.* — Belle   Reuben
Jefferson   Cluter   *m.*   Jones
                                         Aunt
                                      Susannah
                                       Jones

Jim — *m.* — Lila
Williams   Huckaby

Aunt — *m.* — Uncle   Elvira — *m.* — Charles
Tillie   Samuel   Jefferson
                 (*b.*)

Uncle   Aunt — *m.* — Uncle   Aunt
Theo   Flora   Walter   *m.*   Vinnie

Raymond — *m.* — Cora   Grace — *m.* — Lester
Gibbons   Sledge

Freedom

Henry   Jack   Rose   Nancy   Lora
            (*b.*)   Lee   Lee   Lee

White Lilacs

Garden of Eden

IN THE TIME before we knew that we would be driven away, our lives uprooted, and our people scattered, Grandfather Jim Williams spent every spare minute tending his beautiful garden in Freedomtown. He loved that garden, and I loved him. The garden was my favorite place.

"It's the Garden of Eden, Rose Lee," he would tell me, his crinkled brown face shining with quiet pride. "Right here in Freedom."

I knew, of course (I was twelve then, and thought I knew a great deal), that God had created the amazing assortment of trees and bushes and flowers abounding in that Paradise, as colorful and bright as the counterpanes Grandmother Lila stitched for each member of our family. But I also knew whose careful hands set the tender young plants in the rich brown earth, dark as my skin, and nursed them as they sprang up and flourished.

And I knew that many of the plants and bushes and vines had come from the much larger, much finer garden belonging to Mrs. Eunice Bell, where my grandfather worked. He had what we called "toting privileges": he was allowed to take along whatever he had trimmed or thinned or weeded out of Mrs. Bell's garden and plant it in the Garden of Eden. For instance, he had dug up a sucker from the white lilac by Mrs. Bell's kitchen door and coaxed it to take root in his front yard. He laid out a curving path leading to it with odds and ends of broken bricks that my brother Henry brought him from the brickyard, and he built a low picket fence around it so children playing in the neighborhood would not accidentally come too close to his precious white lilac.

"It's very rare," he proudly told those who admired its sweet-smelling blooms. "Purple lilacs are common, but only once in a long while do you come across something like this."

"Fusses over it like it was a child," Grandmother Lila murmured.

"Because its name is most like yours," he
told her soothingly, and she smiled at that.

I remember that the white lilac near Mrs.
Bell's kitchen door was in full bloom on the day
the ladies of the Garden Club of Dillon, Texas,
came to her house for a luncheon. I had gone
along to help Grandfather in Mrs. Bell's garden
that day as I often did, just to be with him, and
I watched the ladies arrive under the porte
cochere where her husband, Mr. Thomas Bell,
parked his Packard automobile. They wore
dainty white gloves and stylish hats to shade
their faces from the harsh Texas sun. They
strolled in their soft leather shoes on the winding brick walks my uncle Theo had laid through
the garden under Grandfather's direction, and
they exclaimed at what they saw.

Mrs. Eunice Bell liked to claim all the credit
for the garden, although I'm sure the club members knew very well that it was Jim Williams
who made it so special. Two or three times a
year Mrs. Bell would step outside of the grand
white house on Oak Street and lead Grandfather around the garden, giving him "guid-
ance," as she called it.

"Jim, I think we'll have shades of pink over

3

yonder on the west side," she'd say with a wave of her hand, "and blues and purples back there toward your shed." But next to the white house itself she would have only white flowers, hostas and creamy lilies and tall irises, set off by their deep green leaves. There were to be no yellow flowers, no orange, or orangy red anywhere. "I've never been fond of those colors, Jim," she would say.

My grandfather would follow her respectfully, nodding as she spoke and murmuring, "Yessum, yessum," and she'd get her shades of pink and her blues and purples wherever she wanted them, and her green and white alongside the house. (In Grandfather's Garden of Eden, the colors were all jumbled up together, and he had added some yellow and orange flowers on his own. I liked that better. It's the way I thought the first Garden of Eden probably was.)

After the ladies had time to admire the flowers and praise Mrs. Bell for creating such a beautiful display, she led them inside — not through the kitchen, of course, where my aunt Tillie was fixing their lunch, but up the broad steps of the veranda that wrapped clear around the side of the house. She ushered them past the pots of white geraniums and through the etched glass door that opened into the east parlor. I was glad to see the ladies pass inside, because that meant I might have time when my work was done to make a few drawings in the lined tablet I kept hidden in the garden shed. I particularly liked to draw flowers.

Just that minute my aunt Tillie leaned out the back door and anxiously beckoned to me. "I need you to serve the lunch," she said as I stepped into the kitchen. "Cora's taken sick."

My cousin Cora, Aunt Tillie's daughter, 'most always served the lunches to company and the dinners to the Bell family — Mr. Thomas Bell and Mrs. Eunice Bell and their daughter, Catherine Jane, who was two years older than me, and their son, Edward, when he was home from college — and any guests who might come by. I had known the Bell family all my life. Mrs. Bell was kind, generous even. She often sent home Catherine Jane's old clothes for me, pretty dresses with lots of wear left in them that Momma said I must be grateful for. But I did not feel easy around any of the Bells except for Catherine Jane.

And now Cora had sent word at the last minute with Uncle Theo that she was feeling poorly, and Aunt Tillie decided I would have to take her place. My mother's whole family worked for the Bells, and now I was included.

Although I helped out in the kitchen sometimes, peeling vegetables or scrubbing the pots when the Bells had a big dinner, I much preferred to be out in the garden with Grandfather Jim. Aunt Tillie had never before asked me to serve in the dining room. Nevertheless, she took hold of my arm and pulled me into the pantry to put on Cora's uniform.

Cora was nineteen, big and robust like Aunt Tillie, and I was kind of a skinny little thing, and that black uniform hung on me like a bedsheet on a pole. Aunt Tillie attacked it with pins, bringing it down to size. She tied the white organdy apron, starched crisp as paper, around my waist with a bow in the back and set the little pleated white coif on top of my springy black hair. She made me put on Cora's black shoes with rags stuffed in the toes to keep them from slopping up and down. Then she pointed to a great big silver tray with ten china bowls filled with creamy soup, which I was to carry out to the ladies whose voices could be heard like soft music on the other side of the swinging door.

"Now, Rose Lee, when you set something down in front of a person, you stand on her *left* side," Aunt Tillie explained. "And when you pick up an empty bowl or a plate or whatever, you stand on her *right* side. Lower Left; Raise Right — that's the rule. Understand?" Without waiting for me to answer, she gave me and the silver tray a firm push through the door. "Go," she said.

The long table was set with white linen mats on the dark, polished wood and linen napkins folded to show the embroidery in the corner. Silver spoons and forks lay alongside flowered china plates. To save my life I could not figure how I was going to follow Aunt Tillie's rule loaded down with that enormous tray. Then I heard Aunt Tillie push open the door a crack. "Set the tray on the sideboard, Rose Lee," she hissed at me.

Sideboard? I looked around and saw a low cupboard that appeared big enough to accommodate the tray, and I lurched toward it, setting the tray and the bowls down with a clatter.

There was a catch in the conversation, and I knew Mrs. Bell was drilling holes in my back with her little blue eyes. My hands were shaking. But then the talk resumed, and I picked up two soup bowls by their graceful curved handles and set them down in front of the two ladies closest to me, one in a hat with so many feathers she looked like a little bird. The other wore no hat and a plain gray suit. Her straight brown hair was fastened back from her face with a pair of combs. Her voice was clear and sharp as ice water, not warm and syrupy, like folks' around here. I continued until nearly all the bowls had been safely delivered.

That's when I saw that Catherine Jane was also at the luncheon. Catherine Jane must be getting awful grown-up, I thought, sitting with her momma's friends. She had the most beautiful blond hair that hung down way below her shoulders, rippling in waves or, when it had just rained or was about to, screwing up in tight curls, although never as tight as mine. Today, in honor of the party, she wore it pulled back with a big white bow. I was careful not to look her in the face when I set the last bowl in front of her, and I thought she was being careful not to look at me.

Now I had ten little china plates left on the tray. What was I supposed to do with them? I was terrified that Mrs. Bell would be upset at this, upset that I wasn't Cora, who surely knew better. I fled back to the kitchen empty-handed and plowed into Aunt Tillie, who had been watching my performance through the crack.

"Rose Lee! You supposed to carry the soup bowls on their saucers and set them down together, just like you do a cup of coffee."

"But there's already a big plate there!"

"On *top* of the big plate, Rose Lee. Big plate, little plate, soup bowl, that's how it goes," she said, demonstrating the order with her hands.

Then she smiled. "White folks use lots of dishes," she said. "You get used to it."

I could feel tears coming. I longed to be out in the garden with Grandfather where I felt at home, digging or drawing, one or the other, but not this!

Aunt Tillie patted my shoulder. "It's all right. They're still busy talking. Now take in these corn muffins and pass them around. Let each lady help herself. From the *left*, Rose Lee!"

I tiptoed back into the dining room, carrying a silver basket lined with a fine linen cloth that had HOT ROLLS stitched on it in pale, satiny letters. Mrs. Bell was too busy listening to her guests to pay me any notice as I slipped around from guest to guest, holding out the basket of muffins. Even Catherine Jane still wasn't looking my way, like I was a complete stranger.

"But it's so obvious, Eunice," said a lady in a large white hat, reaching for a muffin. She had a ring with big diamonds on her finger. "Something has to be done about Freedomtown, and this is the answer."

My ears perked right up when I heard her mention Freedomtown, the neighborhood where I lived. Most all the Negroes of Dillon lived there, except a few colored folks who didn't have regular jobs but got along as best they could and lived in a collection of rickety old shanties to the south of Dillon in a place known as Dogtown. Back then — and this was in 1921 — Freedom, as we called it, was our part of Dillon. There was everything you could want in a town — our colored school and two churches and a grocery store and café and whatever else a town could be expected to have, our own colored doctor, mortician, everything. It just happened that Freedom was right in the middle of Dillon, white people on every side of us. But we all got along fine, long as we colored folks stayed in our part of town except to work. At least that's what I thought.

"I should think those poor Negroes would be happy to leave Freedomtown," said a lady in a lavender dress. "Such a muddy old place with Hickory Creek overflowing every time there's a heavy rain! We'll simply move them to a more appropriate area. But they're like children. They may have to be persuaded that it's for everyone's good."

The silver basket trembled in my hands. Who was this lady to speak about moving people out of Freedom? Move *who?* Move *where?*

Mrs. Bell began to pass around the butter dish, and I rushed back to the kitchen.

"They're talking about us," I whispered anxiously to Aunt Tillie.

"You're not to listen in on other folks' talk," she said sternly. "You're to mind your work and make sure they get served right."

"I couldn't help hearing."

"Don't talk about it now," she warned me. "It's bad business."

Nevertheless, I stood by the door and strained to hear.

"It's important that we get to work on this as soon as possible," said Mrs. Eunice Bell. "Tom's seeing to the legal papers, so that we can talk to people around town about the plan and circulate a petition."

"The site is perfect for a park," said another lady. "Most every other town the size of Dillon in the state of Texas has a city park. Dallas has had several beautiful parks for years now. If we're going to be a growing community and attract the right kind of people, we must have a park here."

"And gardens," Mrs. Bell added. "I can just picture some lovely formal gardens, designed for year-round blooming. Like mine. I'd be happy to help with the planning."

"Don't forget a library," added someone else.

"And a women's club. Certainly the town needs that, to raise the level of culture."

"I frankly cannot think of a single soul who could have the slightest objection to this plan," said Mrs. Bell.

"Except the Negroes," said the lady with the voice like ice water. Mostly I couldn't understand her, but I understood *that*.

And then Mrs. Bell laughed, and the other ladies started to laugh, too, appreciating what must be a joke.

"Did you hear me, Rose Lee?" Aunt Tillie whispered, yanking me away. "Get to work. Their iced-tea glasses must be about empty." I knew by the look on her face that Aunt Tillie had been listening, too.

I swallowed hard and pushed open the door. The pitcher, beaded with sweat, stood on the sideboard, ready for me to carry around to each glass.

"I can imagine that you'd have a different point of view from ours, since you're new to Dillon, Miss Firth," Mrs. Bell was saying in a voice thick and sweet as honey to the lady with ice in her talk. "They probably do things much differently up there in Philadelphia. But this is Texas, after all. Our Negroes aren't like yours. As Madeleine says, they are *childlike*. And I'm sure they'll all be very, very happy to have nice new homes. That's always a source of pleasure, no matter what your race, don't you think?"

She gazed around the table at her guests, who all murmured, "Oh, yes."

"We're not without our Negro problems in the North," the lady explained. I thought she looked a lot younger than the other ladies. "They're arriving by the thousands from all over the South, looking for factory jobs, and they live in the most deplorable conditions."

"Our Negroes wouldn't leave to go North," Mrs. Bell said in a confident tone. "I can say with complete assurance that they're perfectly content here." Then I saw her frown. "Is the ham ready?" she asked, not recognizing it was me, Rose Lee, who was usually out in the garden with mud on my knees, instead of here in her dining room with the sparkling chandelier and the thick carpets.

"Yessum," I said.

Aunt Tillie was waiting for me, scowling. "The bowls? Did you gather up the soup bowls?" I had to rush back and collect them (Raise Right — I remembered at the last second) and I hoped I would not miss something important in their conversation, although I hated what I was hearing and it frightened me.

"What's wrong with you, Rose Lee?" Aunt Tillie scolded when I came back, dirty bowls and unused saucers clattering on the silver tray. But of course she knew — this was just her way of telling me I had to wake up and do things the right way, no matter what was wrong with me. This time I had to carry in a platter of neatly overlapping slices of ham and little bundles of asparagus and a bowl of tiny new potatoes.

Now what was I to do? Uneasily I looked to Mrs. Bell for help, who said only, "Put them down here, please," pointing to the silver trivets in front of her. "I'll serve them."

I knew I should leave then, but stubbornly I stayed, standing motionless to one side where I hoped she wouldn't notice. Catherine Jane noticed, though. I caught her looking at me, and I dropped my eyes and stared at the swirly pattern in the carpet.

— Somehow I managed to get through the rest of the meal. The lady from the North talked about her new job teaching art at the Dillon Academy for Young Ladies, and she told them about the prize-winning roses her mother grew in her garden in Philadelphia. The subject changed to roses. There was no more about Freedomtown. I served the dessert pudding and carried in the silver coffeepot and matching sugar bowl and cream pitcher, glad that Mrs. Bell preferred to pour the coffee into the delicate china cups herself.

The ladies carried their coffee onto the veranda, and Aunt Tillie told me she didn't need me to stay and dry the china and silver as she washed it — afraid I'd break something, I guess.

I was relieved to be out of that house and back in the garden. I found Grandfather behind his shed near the vegetable patch where he grew things Aunt Tillie could use in Mrs. Bell's kitchen — garden lettuce, a few tomato vines, some spring onions. When he went into the shed, I followed him. In the stifling darkness, I repeated what I had heard in the dining room. He listened, nodding.

"Can they make us move, Grandfather?"

"I don't know," he said. "Can if they've a mind to, I guess." He was quiet for a while, cleaning his tools.

Something about the way Grandfather answered made me nervous, and after that I had no heart for drawing. The tablet stayed in its hiding place.

Freedom

I WAS AFRAID Aunt Tillie would tell me I was to stay and serve dinner to the Bell family, but then Cora showed up and I was allowed to leave. When our work was finished, Grandfather and I walked home together. I wasn't too old yet to hold onto his hand. We followed the old trolley tracks east on Oak Street, past the fine houses that were Mr. and Mrs. Bell's neighbors', past the courthouse with the clock that chimed the hour loud enough for us all to hear, and north across Brown Street to Freedomtown.

You knew soon as you crossed Brown Street

that you were in a different place. Hickory Creek was still swollen from spring rains. The three streets that ran north and south and the three streets that cut east and west across them were not paved (they were muddy now from where the two branches of Hickory Creek crossed over, but later, as the summer wore on, my bare feet would be buried in warm dust). Most all the houses were small and plain, without a lick of paint, and set close together. Some might say they looked poor, but each and every one had some little bit of something colorful growing in the front yard. Nothing like Grandfather Jim's, but then that was a special case. You could have only one Garden of Eden.

Hand in hand we walked up Logan Street, our main street with Booker T. Washington Colored School at one end by Brown Street and Forgiveness Baptist Church where my whole family belonged clear up at the other end by Academy Street. I must have walked up and down that street hundreds of times in my life, maybe thousands, but that day after I heard that talk at Mrs. Bell's table, I saw it in a way I never did before.

I was born in Freedomtown. So was my mother, but all the old people had a story to tell about how they came to be there. Grandmother Lila was a young girl when her family, the

Huckabys, moved with a group of other families from near Dallas and helped to establish the little settlement in Dillon during Reconstruction, which followed the War Between the States.

Grandfather Jim had a different story: his poppa was a white man who brought his momma who was once a slave woman all the way out here from Virginia. He bought her a piece of land right next to his own farm up near Blue Springs. That white man acknowledged Grandfather as his son all along and gave Grandfather's momma money for him and her other children by him, but then he died young and Grandfather had to move to town to get work to support his mother and sisters.

When Grandfather and Grandmother married, they settled in Freedom, and most of their family still lived there: Aunt Tillie was the oldest, and then Uncle Theo, who was married to Aunt Flora, and then Momma. Uncle Walter, the youngest, was married to Aunt Vinnie.

My grandfather on Poppa's side was part Seminole, but I never knew him. Poppa came from East Texas when he was a boy with his father and an uncle and one of Poppa's brothers, looking for land to farm. Only Poppa ended up staying in Freedom, and the others went on west. His momma stayed back in East Texas and got a new husband. We used to hear now and then from Poppa's youngest sister, who went to college and was a schoolteacher in St. Louis. This Aunt Susannah came to visit us once when I was barely three years old, but I didn't remember her.

"We got all kinds in my family," Poppa used to say, and I knew that idea tickled him.

"Sure do," Momma would reply in a way that made me know she didn't entirely approve of families splitting up, some going, some staying.

My father owned a barbershop, and my mother took in washing for Mrs. Bell and some other white ladies. Momma wanted me to help out with her laundry business, but I disliked that, preferring to do my helping out in Mrs. Bell's garden. She didn't pay me for my work, but Grandfather gave me a little something out of his pocket for the time I spent there. Whenever I was not in school, I could be found at Mrs. Bell's with Grandfather.

Some of the people of Freedomtown worked at the flour mill or the brickyard. Some, like Poppa and a dozen others, had their own businesses. Others worked at the Dillon Academy for Young Ladies, a finishing school for white girls, with fine brick buildings and green lawns just north of Freedomtown. When the wind was right, we could hear their voices in their playing field on the other side of Academy Street, within sight of Forgiveness Baptist Church.

Most of the rest of our people were employed in the homes of rich folks like Mr. and Mrs. Bell on the west side of Dillon, where the houses were very grand and help was needed to clean and cook and serve and take care of the gardens and mind the children. In fact, the rich folks of Dillon could be counted on to give work to most anybody who wanted it. A few, like my brother Henry, refused to work for them, no matter what the job.

"I won't work for them," Henry said. "People like Mr. Tom Bell think they're at least as good as God Almighty Himself."

"And you think it's better to work at the brickyard?" my mother argued with him. "It doesn't pay more. And it's such dirty, dangerous work."

"It's better," he insisted. "At least it's man's work."

Henry was stubborn. There was no telling him anything. He was always arguing with Momma and Poppa, and they were continually fretting about him and discussing him between themselves.

"He doesn't know his place," Momma

would mutter to Poppa. "He's going to get into trouble."

"He knows his place, he just won't accept it," Poppa said. "Henry's not about to accept some white man's idea of what his place is."

He said it half proud, half worried. People in Freedom as a rule didn't speak out the way my brother Henry did. Henry had been a soldier in the War and got sent to France, and he insisted that things had been different there for Negroes and would have been *more* different if the American officers hadn't told the French how to treat colored boys. "I fought for this country," Henry said. "I deserve better."

Momma said he hadn't been the same since he came back. "He got his hopes up," she explained, "and then they were dashed."

It was suppertime as Grandfather Jim and I walked up Logan Street, and I could smell the cooking. Most of the children had been called inside. Otherwise it would have been noisy and hectic with dozens of little kids, including my two young sisters, Lora Lee and Nancy Lee, running around, laughing and playing with the others. I knew them all. Grandmother Lila was a midwife who had delivered most of the babies in Freedomtown, sometimes taking care of them when their mommas went back to work. I remembered when I used to be like that, young and carefree, having only to mind my momma and not worry about a thing except when I was going to have a chance to play with my friends. But today I felt about a hundred years old, ever since I heard those ladies talking at the Garden Club luncheon about how they were going to make us move away from Freedomtown.

If Grandfather's Garden of Eden was my favorite place in Freedom, my next favorite was Grandmother's parlor, where she sat in her big old rocking chair and did her fancywork after whatever baby she was minding had gone to sleep. A second rocking chair was always ready and waiting for a visitor, and I went there whenever I could. That evening when we entered the house she was sitting in her chair with a neighbor's colicky baby who she was caring for. It screeched so loud in spite of the rocking I couldn't hear myself think. I decided to go on up Logan Street to my own house. Grandmother called, "Come back tomorrow, Rose Lee." Grandfather said he'd walk along with me. I wasn't surprised.

Our home was stark by comparison. My parents didn't have time or interest in growing anything we couldn't eat, and the yard behind our plain wooden house was strung with clotheslines like the warp of a loom with only a small garden patch in the corner opposite the privy for a few melons and some okra. Even so, wild hollyhocks stood tall along the veranda, and Grandfather had brought over some petunias to plant by the steps. He couldn't stand to see a yard that wasn't blooming somehow.

My father was busy in his barbershop in the front room of our house. He stayed open most evenings right through the supper hour, when his customers had time after their work was done to sit down for a visit as well as a shave and a haircut. When it was warm, as it was that night, the men waited their turn out on the veranda, tipping straight wooden chairs back against the house wall or lounging on the wide steps, carrying on their talk through the open window with whoever was inside.

I liked to stay around my father's barbershop, listening to the men talk. I overheard lots of interesting stories there, although my mother did not approve. Not the proper place for a young lady, who might hear bad language and other things that weren't intended for her ears, she claimed.

The evening after the Garden Club lunch I stopped in the barbershop before I went on through to tell Momma I was home. A customer was seated in the barber chair, draped with a clean white towel, and another half dozen men waited their turns.

I recognized all of Poppa's customers: Mr. Morgan, the undertaker, said to be the wealthiest man in Freedom. ("Why not?" my grandmother said. "Everybody needs him sooner or later.") Mr. Lipscomb, who owned a boardinghouse. Pastor Mobley, preacher at Forgiveness Baptist Church. Mr. Ross, head janitor at the Academy. Mr. Webster, proprietor of the Sun-Up Café where the men also gathered to sit and talk, cups of coffee in their hands, while the big slow fan turned noisily overhead. Most of the important men of Freedom were waiting while my father snipped away at the undertaker's bowed head.

Grandfather greeted those on the veranda and followed me inside. "Tell them what you heard, Rose Lee," he said.

My mouth went dry, with all of them looking at me. My father's scissors hovered in midair. "They want to move us," I said. "The ladies of the Dillon Garden Club were saying at Mrs. Bell's that they want to make us all move away somewhere so they can turn Freedom into a park."

Mr. Webster swore, the kind of language

my mother didn't approve of and was afraid I'd hear at the barbershop, and then he apologized to me and to the preacher. "What have I been telling you?" Mr. Webster went on, looking from one to the next. "Isn't this exactly the rumor we been hearing and pretending not to hear? And is it not time to believe it, now that this child has brought us the word, and to figure out what it is we're going to do?"

The men muttered. I saw heads nodding.

"What all did you hear them say, Rose Lee?" Poppa interrupted in his soft, growly voice. "Try to remember everything."

Those who were outside crowded into the little shop to listen better. I repeated every detail that came to mind, mentioning this time the lady from up North who spoke in a different way. "She was the only one who thought we might not like to be moved," I told them.

After they had all asked questions and made me repeat everything I already told them, they began to discuss it among themselves, seeming to forget I was there. That was all right—I preferred to listen anyhow.

Poppa whisked Mr. Morgan's face and neck with a soft-bristled brush and shook the hairs off the white towel, and Mr. Morgan stepped down out of the barber chair and Pastor Mobley took his place. But the undertaker didn't leave; he settled into the chair the preacher had been waiting in.

When a new customer arrived, the men made room for him. More came, but nobody left. When there was no more room inside, they clustered outside the open window. They all wanted to discuss the news I had brought concerning the Garden Club and its plans to beautify Dillon by getting rid of us.

"What are we going to do?" asked one of the men.

"We'll make our voices heard," said Poppa in his growly voice. "We'll tell them it's our property, legally bought and paid for, papers to prove it." He pulled himself up straight and proud, and he gripped his scissors like a sword.

"We'll tell them we're not leaving. What can they do about it?"

One of the men, Mr. Ross I think it was, chuckled softly. "Do whatever they've a mind to, Charlie. You know that."

My brother Henry had come through the heavy green curtain that separated the barbershop from the rest of our house and stood with his arms folded across his chest. He was tall and handsome with Indian features like Poppa's.

"We'll fight it, that's what we're going to

do," Henry said in a deep voice like Poppa's, but younger sounding. "We'll do whatever we have to. They have no right."

"Won't do any good to fight it," Mr. Webster said. "You can say all you like, but if they decide to knock down our homes to make their park, then you can bet there will be a park right where we're standing."

The men stayed late, way past the time Poppa generally locked the front door and passed to the other side of the green curtain for the supper Momma had been keeping warm for him. Some agreed with my father — they would fight to save Freedomtown. Others felt it was useless and were mainly concerned about where they would go when they had to leave.

Then my momma came to get me, annoyed that I wasn't helping back in the kitchen, starting off with her usual, "Rose Lee, how many times do I have to tell you —"

"Listen, Momma," I said, made bold by the attention paid me by my father's customers, "this is what I heard." And I repeated the story one more time. I felt proud to be carrying such important news, proud that Poppa was going to make our voices heard and Henry was going to fight, and if I knew Grandfather Jim, he wouldn't be sitting quietly while they chased him out of his own Garden of Eden.

But Momma didn't look as though she was ready for any fight. My mother burst into tears and cried in front of all those men. That was not the only time she cried in the months that followed.

THREE

Special Gift

I WAS DOWN on my knees, digging dandelions out of the grass in Mrs. Bell's back lawn, making sure to get the whole long root so they wouldn't come back, but they always did anyway. In Freedom we just let them come up wherever they wanted to, thinking their little yellow faces were pretty; but Mrs. Bell didn't like them, so out they came.

"Excuse me!" a voice sang out from the other side of the iron picket fence surrounding Mr. Bell's property. "Hello there!"

I straightened up to see who was calling and caught sight of a white lady. It was the white lady from up North who had been at Mrs. Bell's luncheon.

"Hello!" she called again, waving and smiling. I picked myself up and tried to brush the dirt off my hands and knees before I ran over to the fence to see what she wanted.

"Yessum?"

"Good morning," she said, "I'm Miss Emily Firth. I'm an acquaintance of Mrs. Bell's, and she's given me her permission to come out here and sketch." I noticed that her eyes were the color of bluebonnets, and when she smiled, her small white teeth were perfectly even. She held up a large pad of fine white paper and a box of pencils.

"Yessum," I said, sliding looks at that pad and pencil box, wishing they belonged to me.

"What I'd like to do," she explained, "is to make a sketch of you and that man." She nodded toward Grandfather. "Is he a relative of yours? The two of you working in the garden make such a lovely composition."

This surprised me. I knew why she wanted to make pictures of Mrs. Bell's garden, but a picture of a young colored girl and her grandfather? I went to unlatch the gate for her.

"What's your name, please?" she asked. Seemed she didn't recognize me from when I served her lunch the day before.

"Rose Lee, ma'am."

"Nice to meet you, Rose Lee. I won't need to trouble you any more. Please go on with whatever you're doing and pretend I'm not here."

I went back to work on the dandelions, keeping an eye out for Miss Firth. She set up a little folding stool that I hadn't noticed before, a strip of canvas on a wooden frame. She opened her large sketchbook, selected a pencil, and squinted at me. I tried to pay no attention and keep on with my work, but I kept thinking about the lines she was making on the white paper, the almost magical strokes that could create a likeness. What kind of likeness was she making of me?

Then my mind wandered away from Miss Firth and back to Mrs. Eunice Bell and the plans of the Garden Club. When I looked up again, Miss Firth had gone.

The next day she came back. "I always thought our rose gardens in Philadelphia were beautiful," she said, unfolding her little stool, "but I believe your gardens here in Texas are even more spectacular."

I tried to picture Philadelphia on the map hanging on the wall of my school. (I had a good memory for how things looked, including maps.) Philadelphia — I remembered now, over in the corner of Pennsylvania — seemed far away from Dillon, Texas.

Through the morning hours she sketched. It was cooler in the forenoon, and she had, I suppose, learned that this was the time when the light was calmer, the sun not yet so hot, and no insects stirred the air. "Come and see this, Rose Lee," she called to me. She offered me the book, but my hands were dirty and I kept them behind my back. "Wait," she said, "I'll turn the pages for you."

Her drawings were spare and simple, never one line more than was necessary to show what she wanted to show. Her picture of Grandfather and me was as plain as the rest, two figures at work among the flowers. The kneeling figure was both me and *not* me, the bent-over figure was Grandfather but it was also any bent-over old man. We were part of a design.

I thought the picture was beautiful and I told her so, and then because her smile and her eyes were kind, I confessed, "I like to draw, too."

"Really? Will you show me your drawings some time?"

"I have them in the shed," I said, the words flying out of my mouth before I could stop them.

"Well, then, let's have a look right now!" she said gaily.

Feeling embarrassed and shy and wondering what on earth had made me say that, I ran to the shed and reached behind a stack of clay pots and pulled out the cigar box with my stubby lead pencils and my old school tablet. In it were little sketches of the hollyhocks by our veranda, of Grandfather Jim's precious lilac bush with the fence around it, and one I had started but not finished of the county courthouse with the clock and nine cupolas perched like muffins on the roof. My drawings suddenly looked crude to me. They were missing the magic of Miss Firth's drawings.

I was shy about these drawings and kept them mostly a secret. Momma and Poppa knew about my drawing, but I didn't show them the tablet and they didn't ask. My sisters wouldn't care, and I didn't let my brother see them, either. Nor did I bother to tell my friends Bessie and Lou Ann about my drawings. I didn't want to *talk* about it — it was just something I *did*.

Once in a while I showed them to Grandfather. He would gaze at each one, head cocked to one side, and say things like, "Yes, that's it, all right," and "I think you need to fix something here somehow."

Grandmother Lila knew that I liked to draw the way she liked to embroider and crochet. She was making me a counterpane, a big white bedsheet with a brown wicker basket stitched in the center, overflowing with pink and blue and purple flowers with yellow centers and green leaves, surrounded by ribbon bows waving like flags.

"I'll crochet a blue edging all around, Rose Lee," she promised. "This will be yours someday, when you're all grown-up and have a home of your own."

When I was younger, she had tried to teach me how to embroider flowers, petals in lazy daisy stitch around a center of French knots, chain-stitched stems and satin-stitched leaves. But I was impatient with the needle and embroidery floss and the hoop that held the cloth stretched tight, and I never could stand to have a thimble on my finger.

"I'd rather draw the flowers, Grandmother," I told her. "Like this." I took the pencil she used to write her shopping list, and on a scrap of paper I drew the morning glories that trailed over her back fence.

Grandmother studied my drawing carefully. "God has given you a special gift, Rose Lee. Do good with it."

After that she didn't coax me to practice lazy daisies and French knots. Sometimes I showed her what I had drawn, and she would study the sketch and nod seriously. "A special gift," she'd remind me.

It was an entirely different thing, showing my pictures to Miss Firth. I gave her the tablet and watched as she slowly turned the pages, studying each one. I tried to read her face to see what was going on in her mind, but I could not. When she handed the tablet back to me, she was smiling.

"You are very talented, Rose Lee. Do you know that?"

"No, ma'am," I said, but I couldn't hold back my grin, remembering what Grandmother Lila had said. "I just do what I like to do."

"And you do it very well. Now then," she said, snapping off the words in a businesslike way, "I'm planning to begin a small class of private pupils this summer, and I'd like very much to have you join the class. Would you like that? There would be no charge. With your parents' permission, naturally."

I was astonished. I had not expected anything like this, and I hardly knew what to do or say, except to stand there, squeezing my hands together and grinning. But then I remembered my manners, to thank her and to say oh yes ma'am, I did want to have her teach me, and yes ma'am, I was sure it would be all right with my parents.

Now for the first time since the Garden Club luncheon I had something to fill my mind besides the future of Freedomtown. But that shows you how little I knew about the people of Dillon, and for that matter, how little Miss Emily Firth knew about them, too.

FOUR

Lessons

THAT NIGHT after the barbershop closed, we sat at the kitchen table. Nancy Lee and Lora Lee were in their nightclothes, chattering about whatever childish thing was on their minds, and Henry mopped up his third plate of greens with a piece of Momma's corn bread. Poppa had news.

"Pastor Mobley came by today," he told us. "He says white folks are circulating a petition."

I didn't understand what a petition could do.

"It means, Rose Lee," Poppa explained, "that if enough people sign this piece of paper, then the people of Dillon will vote to decide if we can stay in our homes, or if we must move away. They won't say that's what it means, though. They'll say they're voting to raise money to buy up land for a city park. But the land they intend to buy is ours."

"But can't we vote against it?" I asked, and Henry broke his silence with a harsh laugh. I could sense a whole ocean of anger roiling beneath the surface of his calm. I loved my brother and looked up to him. Poppa said he was smart and he hoped some day Henry would go to college like Aunt Susannah — "He'd be the second one in the family," Poppa often said proudly. But Henry's anger often frightened me. Like my parents, I was scared it would get him into trouble.

"Could if they let us. Legally a black man can vote just the same as a white man can. Fifteenth Amendment to the Constitution of the United States. But they not going to *let* us. They going to make sure we *don't* by their various and considerable powers of persuasion."

Henry was talking more and more like a preacher, I thought. What did he mean by "various and considerable" whatever it was?

But then Momma cut in. "Women, too, Henry," she said. "Don't forget the women have the vote now, too."

But Henry ignored Momma. "There's more of them than there is of us, no matter how you count," Henry said. "Even if there wasn't, they'd figure it out somehow. It's time we do something, get ourselves together, and take a stand. Why do you think I went down to Dallas and joined up with UNIA?"

"I told you I don't want you messing with that bunch of radicals, Henry," Poppa warned. "That Marcus Garvey is nothing but trouble."

"What's so radical about Mr. Garvey telling me I'm good as any white man and equal to him in every way? Maybe it's about time black folks around here *get* radical," Henry insisted, "or all we'll ever *have* is trouble."

I had heard them argue about this before, nobody ever getting anywhere. Henry had joined up with this United Negro Improvement Association and kept telling us that the man to follow was the founder of the association, Marcus Garvey, while Poppa and the other men of Freedom said the ideas of Booker T. Washington were good enough for them, which is why they named our school after him. Mr. Washington, we were taught, believed the way to equality was through training for jobs.

"All old Booker ever cared about was training Negroes for jobs, to serve Ol' Massa better," Henry would argue. "Mr. Garvey knows we got to go for a lot more, that we need to form our own nation. He favors going back to Africa, to Liberia, where we can be free men."

"Insisting on our right to stay here where we belong is where we got to take our stand," Poppa said now. "Never mind going to Africa. My home is right here. This house, this piece of ground."

I leaned one way then the other, depending on who was talking. I wasn't exactly sure where Liberia was, which part of Africa.

"You better start packing, Poppa," Henry's voice was rough, almost to choking, with anger, " 'cause you gonna lose." I feared that he was right.

Poppa sighed, and Henry shoved back his chair and stomped out, which was how most of these arguments ended. This was the time I had been planning to tell Momma and Poppa about Miss Firth and her art class, and how she had invited me to be in it, but I had to wait for things to calm down. And before I could say anything, Poppa turned to me.

"Rose Lee," he began, "I'm going to ask you to do something I have an idea you won't want to do."

There was hardly anything Poppa ever asked me that I didn't want to do; not like Momma, who always wanted me to do things

I'd rather not, like taking down the wash from the lines in the backyard, or looking after my little sisters. "What, Poppa?"

"From now on you're to take Cora's place at Mrs. Bell's. Now that school's out, you'll have time."

I set down my glass and stared at him, hoping I hadn't heard right. "How come?"

"Because Cora is still feeling poorly, and she needs to stay off her feet."

"But she's big and strong!" I protested. "And she's been doing it and knows how to do it, and I don't!"

"Cora's going to have a baby," Momma explained. "And you can learn. Aunt Tillie's going to teach you everything you need to know. She said you did real good the other day when you took Cora's place."

"But there must be somebody else," I argued, although I knew it wasn't going to make a bit of difference. Their minds were made up.

They didn't understand how much I hated serving at table. Leave me out in the garden and I was happy, but don't ask me to go inside that grand house where everything was too costly, too fragile, too subject to mistake or carelessness. I recalled my misery with the soup bowls: Lower Left; Raise Right.

"Besides," Momma added, "you'll get paid."

That put a different light on it. "How much?"

"A dollar a week, after you learn everything, and your lunch. You know we can use the extra money."

"Yes, ma'am." I wondered if I'd be allowed to keep any of it. I wanted to buy a real sketchpad, and maybe some colored pencils. Then I went ahead and told them what Miss Emily Firth had said. How could they say no, especially if I agreed to be the serving maid?

"Huh," Momma said. "Did this fine lady say where her art classes are to take place? And who all's to be in it?"

"No. She just said it wouldn't cost anything, and she'd get your permission."

"Don't get your hopes up too high, Rose Lee, and see them dashed."

Poppa cleared his throat. "About the Bells," he said. "There is something else."

I waited to hear what this something else was.

"You keep your ears open, all right? Pay attention like you did before, and hear what's said and remember it all. You understand, baby?"

"You mean about their plans to get rid of Freedom," I said in a flat voice, trying to keep the shake out of it.

He nodded.

"You want this child to be a spy, in other words," Momma said, and I understood from her tone that this was something they didn't agree on. For once I was on Momma's side.

"Call it what you want, Elvie. But if we're to make our plans, we need to know *their* plans. Maybe they'll talk in front of her, like they did before. It will help. Every bit will help." Poppa turned to me. "Well, Rose Lee?"

"I'll do it, Poppa," I said, dreading it but thinking maybe Henry was right: we had to resist or go someplace else, and since I didn't want to go to Africa, I had to do what I could to help.

The next day Aunt Tillie brought me Cora's black uniform, cut down to size. "Make sure the apron's always clean and starched," she said. "Mrs. Bell is real fussy about that. And you got to pay attention so I can teach you things before you go making mistakes like you did last time."

So now there were lessons in Mrs. Eunice Bell's dining room every morning after Aunt Tillie had given the family their breakfast and we had washed the dishes and shined up the kitchen together. I had to learn the name and use of every kind of knife, fork, and spoon, every kind of plate, bowl, cup, and saucer, every kind of tablecloth, napkin, and place mat, every kind of glass and goblet. In addition there were platters and covered dishes and gravy boats and special silver forks and spoons and dippers to go with them. All the dishes were displayed in the china closet with the curving glass front, the linens were laid in particular drawers in the sideboard, and the silver wrapped in soft cloths and kept in a wooden box lined with felt. It would be my job to set the table for each meal as soon as Mrs. Bell let us know how many were expected.

That part was not so hard, once I learned how Mrs. Bell wanted everything. For instance, I had to remember that the china plates were to be put on the table right side up. At home Momma taught me to set the table with the plate turned upside down so it wouldn't get dusty. You turned it over when you sat down to eat, right after the blessing. But Mrs. Bell didn't worry about dust because the street outside her house was paved and there was grass everywhere, not plain dirt that was always mud about to turn to dust or dust about to turn to mud.

Serving the food was a different story. Sometimes all Mrs. Bell wanted was for me to carry in the bowls of vegetables and platters of meat and to set them on the table and let folks pass the food around among themselves. Then Mrs. Bell would say, "You may go now . . ." trailing off because she was still thinking of Cora and never could seem to remember my name. She called that "family style," but it was not like our family, where Momma dished up whatever was in the cook pot with a big spoon and, reaching across, scooped a helping onto our plates.

Other times I was to carry the bowls and platters around one by one to each person and hold it so they could help themselves, or sometimes even to serve the slice of ham or beef onto the person's plate, the silver serving fork trembling in my hand. That's what she called "company style," and for that I was to wear white cotton gloves, which made everything much slipperier.

I was so scared those first days as a maid! Even more scared than I was on the day of the lunch for the ladies of the Dillon Garden Club, because that had happened so quick that I had no time to let fear grow inside me. Now I knew that I had reason to be scared, and I was — always afraid of doing something wrong and upsetting Mrs. Bell. There was a danger of bursting into tears, weeping in front of everybody.

Usually I served the whole family — Mr. Tom and Mrs. Eunice Bell, and Catherine Jane who looked at me oddly or else pretended I wasn't there at all, and also Edward Bell, their son who was Henry's age, just graduated from the university in Austin, Texas. Sometimes some of Edward's school friends came home with him, all of them clattering up to the third floor of the house and playing pool and other games until it was time for supper. Dinner, they called it here.

Besides the family and friends there were often guests. Most of the important people in Dillon came to dine because Mr. Thomas Bell was a lawyer and businessman and a member of the Dillon City Council and an official in his church. It was Mrs. Eunice Bell's notion that the table should always be set for the family and the expected guests, plus two extra places in case somebody came by and could be invited to stay for dinner.

I was glad nobody extra came for dinner during my first week as a maid. I was still too nervous. I knew if I was to do as I promised Poppa — what he called "paying attention," and what Momma called "spying" — I would have to stop worrying about service plates and salad forks and Lower Left and Raise Right and become smooth and easy at what I was doing.

This left me almost no time to think about Miss Emily Firth and her art classes. But once in a while, it did come to mind.

FIVE

Catherine Jane

I HAD BEEN SERVING Mrs. Bell's table for a week or two when Catherine Jane came out to the kitchen after dinner was over. I was getting ready to wash the dishes. Aunt Tillie had gone home early to see to Cora, and I was not looking forward to this task.

"Rose Lee, what are you doing here? Where's Cora?" she asked. "I thought you were supposed to work out in the garden with Jim."

"Cora can't do it anymore," I explained. "She's feeling poorly. They sent me to learn to do it in her place."

Catherine Jane seemed satisfied with that.

"We haven't had a good talk for a long time," she said.

I nodded. "I know."

I WAS ABOUT five years old—that would have made her seven—when Catherine Jane discovered me in the garden following after Grandfather, carrying a trowel or something meant to help him.

"What's your name?" she had asked, and I told her.

"Come on, Rose Lee," she said. "I like your name. You sound like a flower. Come inside and I'll show you my dolls."

Her mother was gone visiting, Catherine Jane said, and she had been left in the care of the cook, my aunt Tillie. But Aunt Tillie was busy fixing dinner, and Catherine Jane had slipped outside to the garden.

Catherine Jane took me in by the side door—the one with etched glass—so Aunt Tillie wouldn't see us, and led me on tiptoe through the east parlor. I remember the velvet-covered sofa with silk fringe and tables with carved legs and a thick carpet with many different colors. Lace curtains hung at the windows. There was a beautiful black piano with the lid raised, and next to it stood a tall wooden box painted gold and decorated with fat pink babies with feathery wings carrying garlands of roses. "What's that?" I asked.

"It's a Victrola. It makes music," Catherine Jane had whispered. "I'll play it for you later."

I gazed openmouthed at the chandelier above the dining-room table, hundreds of sparkling prisms catching the light and breaking it into colors that splashed on the walls. Then I moved slowly after her into the front hall that had a big clock that chimed. Catherine Jane urged me along, impatient to get me up to her room.

We climbed the winding staircase past little silk-shaded lamps attached to the walls. At the top of the stairs, Catherine Jane stopped suddenly and looked at me with her eyes narrowed, a look that I was to see often.

"You're dirty, Rose Lee. Very dirty. You need a good washing."

Next thing I knew, I was in a room the size of Momma's kitchen, the walls and floor all covered in gleaming white tile. In one corner a big tub stood on feet with claws. Catherine Jane turned a knob and showed me how water gushed out of a spout and into the tub. But I was most interested in a large china bowl set on the floor about the same height as a chair. The bowl had water in it.

"That's a toilet, Rose Lee," Catherine Jane said. "I guess you've never seen one of these before. Here, I'll show you how it works."

With that she lifted her skirt, pulled down her panties, hoisted herself up on the bowl, and peed right into the water. While I stared, she pulled her panties up again and yanked on a chain. Water from a tank near the ceiling whooshed down through a pipe and the peed-in water drained out the bottom.

"Now you," she said. Obediently I took my turn.

Next she filled the basin with warm water and helped me wash my hands with pretty soap that smelled nice, and we dried them on a thick white towel. We scampered out of the white room and down the hall to her bedroom.

Catherine Jane showed me her dolls, a whole shelf of them, all beautifully clothed in dresses trimmed with lace and ribbons and dainty hats and tiny leather shoes. We arranged two of them on chairs at a small table and fed them pretend tea and cakes.

Then, because she said she was really getting too old to play with dolls anymore, Catherine Jane allowed me to pick a book from another shelf, and we climbed up on her bed with a pink ruffled counterpane, and she read to me. The book was called *A Child's Garden of Verses*.

"You want to see the rest of the house?" she asked, suddenly bored and shutting the book. I said I did, although I could have gone on forever holding her blue-eyed doll and listening to her read those poems.

We tiptoed out of her room, listening at the top of the stairs to make sure no one was checking up on us, and then she led me silently from room to room.

"My mummy and daddy's room," she whispered, pushing open the door. There was an enormous bed and a dressing table with a tall mirror and a collection of delicate glass bottles. We peered into the closet, reverently touching Mrs. Bell's silk and linen dresses and her shoes with high heels and pointed toes. Before we got too scared to stay any longer, Catherine Jane even opened a drawer in her mother's bureau and let me gaze at the silk underthings and sniff the gentle perfume that floated in the air around them.

Next was her brother Edward's room, the walls covered with maps and a big Confederate flag. She showed me a crystal radio set he had built himself, but I didn't care about that. Two more rooms, kept especially for company, were not as interesting.

Then we climbed another, narrower set of stairs to the third floor, and she opened the door to a huge game room where she and Edward and their friends were sent to play, and a smaller room she called a "smoker" where her father took his friends after dinner to smoke the cigars and cigarettes that Mrs. Bell wouldn't allow anywhere else in the house. The stale air smelled bad.

Finally she led me out onto a balcony high above the front door and pointed toward the town square. "There's the courthouse," she said. "You can tell what time it is by looking at the clock in the tower. Mummy sometimes sends me up here to check and make sure her hall clock is keeping the right time."

"I live over there," I told her, pointing toward Freedom. "On the other side of the clock."

Then she spotted a taxi coming from down the street. "My mother," she said breathlessly and yanked me back inside. "Now, Rose Lee, we have to figure out a way to get you out of here *undetected.*"

Sometimes I didn't understand all the words Catherine Jane used, but I caught the excitement in her voice. Clutching each other and giggling with terror, we ran down the stairs to the second floor just as the front door opened.

"Hurry, Rose Lee," she whispered, motioning dramatically. "The secret stairway."

The steep backstairs were enclosed and dark like a closet, and we crept down, feeling our way along, until we reached a door near the kitchen. I could hear Aunt Tillie singing softly. Catherine Jane opened the door and shoved me through it and then shut it quickly behind me. I found myself in the pantry. When Aunt Tillie turned around, I was alone.

"What're you doing there, child?" my aunt demanded.

I didn't know what to say. Probably I wasn't supposed to be in the house. Why else would Catherine Jane have deserted me here? "Nothing," I said.

Aunt Tillie jerked me by my arm, swatted me once but not hard on my backside, and sent me outside to find Grandfather. "Don't you go poking around in this house, Rose Lee!" she warned. "You have no business here!"

I cried a little, to show her I understood and wouldn't do it again. But I knew I would if I ever got a chance.

The next day I saw my friends Bessie and Lou Ann. I was bursting to tell them about the wonderful white room with all the water, even water to carry away your pee. But when my story came tumbling out, they stared at me doubtfully.

"No such thing, Rose Lee," Bessie said soberly. "Even white folks don't have any such thing like that." I was disappointed not to be believed.

After that, Catherine Jane and I often played together. We were just children then, hollering and laughing while we played hide-and-seek and other games that she thought up and I went along with, because she was older and because it was her home. Whenever Mrs. Eunice Bell went out visiting or to a club meeting, and Catherine Jane was home alone, she came to the garden looking for me and smuggled me into the house. It was part of the thrilling game for her to show me things no little colored girl was supposed to see and then to smuggle me out again. When her mother was at home, we sometimes played in Grandfather's garden shed. Catherine Jane called it our hideout, and since we had no toys there, everything we did was pretend. Because she thought it was "my" shed, that was as close as I ever got to having Catherine Jane come to play at my house.

Then we got older, and the secret visits inside the house ended. The shed stopped being so interesting, too. I wondered if Catherine

Jane ever thought about those hours we had spent together when we were children, long before I began to carry the food to her table.

We hadn't paid much attention then to her being white and me being colored. It seemed all right to be friends when I was a little girl tagging along after Jim, the colored gardener. But now we were older, and I knew it wasn't the same and figured she knew it, too. The color of our skin made all the difference. Maybe Catherine Jane's parents decided we should not be friends anymore, although I doubt they knew how close we were. Or maybe it was Catherine Jane's idea, now she was fourteen and becoming a grown-up lady, attending her momma's Garden Club luncheons, and I was twelve and had to hold the platter while she decided which piece of ham she wanted. That's why we hadn't had a good talk for a long time.

SHE FOUND HERSELF a place to sit on Aunt Tillie's resting stool and watched me for a minute or two while I plunged the glasses into hot, soapy water, then two rinses, and set them on a clean white cloth to drain. "I'm going to take art lessons," she told me. "Soon as school's finished, I'll be going two mornings a week."

"You are?" I blurted out, and then I caught

myself. I realized that if Catherine Jane was to be in the art class, then I was not. "That's nice," I said. I made myself busy with the glasses.

"It's that Miss Firth who's teaching it, the northern lady who came to Mother's luncheon as Mrs. Emmett's guest. Remember her? The one with the funny way of talking?"

"I remember." I licked my lips and tasted salt and jealousy.

"Well, she's the new art teacher at the Academy and she's started a summer class to be held over on the campus. Since Mother knows how much I like to draw, she's letting me go."

"Uh huh." Since when did Catherine Jane like drawing so much, I wondered? It was me who used to show her how to do a few simple flowers. Easy things.

"We think it's best not to tell Daddy about it, though. Daddy says he's heard that Miss Firth's a Philadelphia Quaker and her family were abolitionists back during the War Between the States. That means troublemakers, in case you don't know, Rose Lee. I know for a fact they used to hang abolitionists here in our part of Texas."

Of course I knew about the abolitionists. We learned about them in our school, told by Miss Simpson that we had those people to thank for our freedom. Well, if Miss Firth's people were abolitionists, it meant nothing to me, because it was plain that I was not to be in her art class after all. I should not have been surprised. We colored folks were never allowed to mingle with white folks, not on trains or in schools or parks or restaurants or in any public place. Miss Simpson called them Jim Crow laws. She said they didn't have such laws in the North. Miss Firth must not have known about those laws when she first invited me to her art class. I tried not to feel too disappointed—dashed, as Momma said—but I was unsuccessful. For one awful moment I just wanted to plunge Catherine Jane's beautiful blond head into that pan of dishwater.

"When you're not so busy," Catherine Jane said, "I'll show you some of my drawings."

"All right," I said. But I knew that if Catherine Jane invited me up to her room today the way she used to, I would not go.

SIX

Dinner Party

"COMPANY COMING tonight," Aunt Tillie informed me one Saturday afternoon early in June. "Big important people, seems like. You'll get to see the mayor of Dillon himself, Rose Lee."

She was fixing a special roast, and I was to make sure the silver carving knife was sharp and the silver fork was propped next to it on a crystal knife rest beside Mr. Tom Bell's place. There were always those little details to keep in mind, not to slip up on.

When they had finished their fruit cup and I had taken away the tall silver goblets in which the fruit had been served, I carried in the roast of beef and set it on a trivet in front of Mr. Bell and stepped aside. Everybody watched while Mr. Bell stood up and speared the roast and began carving thick slabs of meat, and I glanced around the table.

Edward was present, dressed up in a linen suit and starched collar, but not Catherine Jane, who was probably still considered too young for such a dinner. I recognized two of the ladies who had attended the Garden Club lunch. Next to the one who had worn the feathered hat sat a man with bushy white side-whiskers and a gold watch chain draped across his bulging stomach. This, I thought, must be the mayor. There were other men in starched collars, and ladies wearing pretty dresses and perfume, but the fat man with the whiskers occupied my attention. Miss Emily Firth was not present.

Then Mr. Bell signaled that I was to offer the platter of beef slices, running with red juice, to each guest. "Well," boomed the whiskery man, his fat-sausage fingers wrapped around one of Mrs. Bell's best crystal water glasses, "it looks as though our little project is moving along according to plan. Am I right, Wesley?"

I saw him wink at the man seated across the table from him, a man I heard Mrs. Bell introduce as Dr. Thompson. I was thinking that this tall, thin man with his dark hair pomaded to a gleam like polished wood was a doctor like our Dr. Ragsdale. But the conversation that followed led me to a different conclusion.

"I'd be pleased to say a few words about that," said this Dr. Thompson, leaning forward just as I stepped up to fill his water glass. This was one of the rules I had to learn: when the glass is half empty, fill it up again. Not before, not after. "Before, and you be making a pest of yourself," Aunt Tillie had explained, "running back and forth like you watering flowers. After, and Mrs. Bell be giving you bad looks." I didn't want to risk any bad looks.

"Do tell us, Wesley," Mrs. Bell said with her company smile. "I know that we are seriously considering sending our Catherine Jane up to the Academy when she's ready in a year or two, but I for one would be just the tiniest mite concerned about her safety and welfare under the current conditions over yonder."

Safety and welfare? Current conditions? What was she talking about?

"I sincerely believe we can continue to attract a finer type of young lady to the Academy once the, uh, *present inhabitants* have been removed and relocated," Dr. Thompson replied smoothly. Now that he was the center of attention at the table, I understood that he was a big somebody at the Dillon Academy for Young Ladies. "If the, uh, present inhabitants were permitted to remain where they are, then I think sensitive, astute parents like yourselves certainly have some justifiable concerns."

His words hit me with a shock, as though he had thrown the glass of ice water I had just poured him right in my face. He was talking about us! I turned quickly and went to the sideboard to set down the water pitcher and steady myself.

Some of his words, some of his way of speaking, were too rich for me, but I understood what was meant. The people of Freedom were the "present inhabitants" he was worried about, the "current conditions." It made me half sick: they thought we were a danger!

Surely they knew I was right there in the same room. But they went on talking about Freedomtown as if I was not present, or at least not visible. Then I noticed that the basket of hot rolls was nearly empty, and I seized it and fled to the kitchen. I wanted to throw myself into Aunt Tillie's thick arms and bury my face in her bosom, but there was no time for that. Dr. Thompson was speaking again. I hunched close by the door and listened.

"I see great days ahead for our Academy," Dr. Thompson said. "I predict it will continue to grow and that benefactors will come forth to donate large sums of money for new buildings — a bigger library, which is so sorely needed, and a greenhouse, and a recital hall with a fine imported European piano. And my vision is possible because the people of Dillon are prepared to rid our city of the blight, to eradicate the squalor, of that area known familiarly as Freedomtown."

I gasped.

"Rose Lee," Aunt Tillie said sternly.

"I believe Mayor Dixon has some good news in that regard," said Mr. Tom Bell.

"Hush," I whispered to Aunt Tillie, which I knew was rude, but I couldn't help it. "Listen." Aunt Tillie came and stood beside me, and we both listened.

"A petition has been successfully circulated," the mayor told the guests. "We've got all the signatures we need — one hundred and fifty of them — asking for a vote on a bond issue to buy up the properties owned by the Negroes. The vote is set for thirty days from today. We go to the polls on Tuesday, July fifth, the day after our annual town barbecue. Plenty of chance for those of us who support the idea of a city park to speechify and persuade any who might still need convincing. What do you say, Tom?"

"Remember," Mr. Bell said, "only property owners and their wives are eligible to vote on a bond issue. I urge all of you here tonight to go out and knock on doors to make sure everyone who is eligible will get out and vote in favor of it."

"It is not an exaggeration to say," said Dr. Thompson, "that the future of Dillon depends on the outcome."

Everybody clapped, and then the guests began talking among themselves. I turned to Aunt Tillie, still holding the silver basket.

"Let 'em do without their damn rolls," Aunt Tillie growled and stalked back to the table where she was laying out the dessert.

Somehow I managed to get through the rest of the meal, hoping they'd decide to take their coffee on the veranda so that I could escape. This time, though, it was different: the men all went upstairs to Mr. Bell's smoker on the third floor to continue their discussion with cigars. The ladies decided, because of the heat, to have iced tea in the parlor.

"You go on home now," Aunt Tillie said when I went back to the kitchen to help her. "I'll finish up here. Somebody waiting for you out there." She jerked her head toward the garden.

I ran outside, expecting the "somebody" to

be Grandfather Jim. He sometimes liked to come back late in the evening when it was cooler. Instead I found Catherine Jane sitting on the steps outside the kitchen door.

"Let's go back to the shed," she said, standing up and brushing off her light-colored skirt. "All right?"

"All right," I said reluctantly and followed her through the garden.

I unlatched the door of the shed and propped it open, and we sat down side by side on the doorstep, the way we used to. "I heard what they were saying tonight," Catherine Jane said, tucking her skirt carefully beneath her legs.

"You did?"

"I was standing in the hallway. Eavesdropping," she added, "which Mother says is bad manners, but I don't care. She said I was too young to come, and I wanted to know what they were talking about. Usually grown-up talk is boring, but not tonight."

So she heard the same thing I did! I waited for her to say more.

"Rose Lee, they're going to make y'all move, aren't they?"

"Seems they're going to try."

"What are you going to do? Where will you go?"

"I don't know," I said.

"Miss Firth, the art teacher, came by to visit earlier," Catherine Jane said. "I heard her talking to Mother about you people. She said it was wrong, trying to force the Negroes to move away. Mother tried to be polite, explaining it was for the good of the community, and y'all would be much happier in new homes anyway. Is that true, Rose Lee? That you'd be happier?"

"No, Catherine Jane, it's not. My grandmother says she's not leaving, no matter how the vote goes. 'They'll have to carry me off with their own hands,' she says. My poppa and my grandfather say they intend to stand up for their rights, but they don't really believe it'll do any good. And my momma, she cries a lot." I was close to tears then myself. I didn't mention Henry and his insistence that we had to resist or else go to Africa. And suddenly I was afraid that I had already said too much.

"Miss Firth said nobody asked y'all."

"She's right. Nobody did."

"Well, that's what I thought, too, but I couldn't say a word. You know Mother! She always says I'm too young to know about such things. But here's what I wanted to tell you, Rose Lee: afterwards Mother talked to Daddy about it, how this Yankee lady came in here trying to tell us how to mind our business, someone who had been brought to our house as a guest Mother had been generous enough to include. Daddy said Miss Firth's like the carpetbaggers after the War Between the States. And then he said he was going to tell his friend Dr. Wesley Thompson that a certain art teacher is going around talking against the very thing Dr. Thompson is in favor of, for the good of the school. So now I'm afraid Miss Firth is going to lose her job at the Academy, and of course that's the end of my art lessons."

I stood up and stepped away from the shed. I could see the lights shining up in the third-floor smoker. "I'm sorry if you can't take art lessons, Catherine Jane," I said. "But at least you are not in any danger of losing your home."

Now I *knew* I had said too much. Catherine Jane sat on the doorstep, her mouth a big O that I could see even in the dark. Maybe she'd tell her poppa what I said and he'd make sure I lost my job, too. I didn't care. I just wanted to go home and take off my uniform and tell Poppa everything I had heard.

"I'm sorry," said Catherine Jane.

I stared at her, her pale face and pale hair ghostly in the darkness.

"I mean it, Rose Lee. I'm sorry. That was a stupid thing I said. I don't want you to have to move."

"All right," I said.

"I'd better go back inside."

"Uh huh. I better get on home."

And then she slipped back into the big white house, and I shut up the shed and let myself out through the iron gate. I ran all the way home in my bare feet to tell them my news. But it turned out they had news for me, too.

SEVEN

Aunt Susannah

I TOLD THEM everything I could remember: what the mayor said, and what Dr. Wesley Thompson said. I couldn't recall all their words exactly, but I did remember the important ones: *current conditions* and *present inhabitants*, and *ridding the city of blight* and *eradicating squalor*. All of it meant *us*.

"Bad enough what all they said about us," I said. "But they got all the people signed up on their petition to have a vote. The vote is to be in a month, the day after their Fourth of July picnic. And they are going to go around knocking on doors and making sure people vote the right way. *Their* way. In order to get rid of the present inhabitants."

When I finished telling, everybody did what they always did: Poppa sighed — a long, hopeless, helpless sigh — and slapped the palm of one hand with the fist of the other. Momma cried. And Henry argued.

"They can't do this to us!" Henry insisted.

"Where'd you get that idea, son? Course they can do anything they want to, because they're white and we're black. Or did you forget that while you were over there in France?"

And then Mrs. Morgan, my friend Bessie's momma, came by to talk about some business with my momma (they were planning a fish fry on the Fourth of July to raise some money for their club) and naturally Mrs. Morgan wanted to know all about what I had heard at Mrs. Bell's dinner, and Momma said after she left that everybody in Freedom would hear about it by sunup tomorrow because she was the talkingest woman in town.

"That's why her husband's an undertaker," Poppa said. "At least his customers don't talk back."

And Momma laughed. It was good to hear her laugh like that, because she hadn't been laughing much since Freedom's troubles began.

The thing about Freedom was we were more

than neighbors, more than friends. We were more like a big family, even though there were fusses and disagreements from time to time, just like in any family. I'd always assumed it was always going to be that way, that nothing would change. But now I could see that things *would* change. Still, I thought that if we had to move away, we'd all move together. We'd find a spot and everybody would go there, and Freedomtown would be just like before.

"Not going to be just like before," Poppa said. "Never going to be just like before, Rose Lee."

"Why not?"

"Because not everybody going to want to go. Some's going to have other ideas, other plans. Raymond Gibbons was by today for a haircut." Raymond Gibbons was my cousin Cora's husband. Aunt Tillie didn't think much of him, I knew, but I liked him fine because he played the banjo. "He's talking about moving back up to Oklahoma where he's got kin."

"Oklahoma!" I was astonished. "And taking Cora with him?"

Poppa laughed. "Well, yes, I believe so. And the baby, too, soon as it's born."

"Does Aunt Tillie know?" I asked.

"No, and don't you go telling her yet. I shouldn't have said this in front of you, Rose

Lee, I see that. Let Raymond and Cora talk to her about it."

"She's gonna be upset," I predicted.

"Lots of people going to be upset before this is done," Momma said. She was tracing her finger over the bunches of red cherries printed on the oilcloth covering the table. I noticed again what long, pretty fingers she had. How could she sit there like that, so calm, when Cora might be leaving? I slid off my chair and started for the back door, just to be moving around.

"Sit down, Rose Lee," Poppa said. "We got some good news you'll be glad to hear."

"Good news?" I sat down at my place at the table again. "What's the good news?"

"Your aunt Susannah is coming to see us," Momma said.

"My baby sister, all the way from St. Louis, going to spend some time this summer with us. Won't that be fine?" Poppa explained, although I didn't need to have Aunt Susannah explained. We kept a picture of her in our sitting room next to one of Henry looking proud and serious in his army uniform. In her picture, she's all dressed up in a black robe and some kind of a flat-topped hat that she wore when she graduated from college, before she went up to St. Louis to be a schoolteacher. Sometimes I used to stand and stare at that picture and wonder if such a thing could ever happen to me, that I'd go off to college and end up in some big city with a job and fine clothes and a house of my own. Maybe even a car. I figured this Aunt Susannah had all those things. The last time she came to see us, I was only about three, too little to remember.

"When's she coming?"

"Soon," Momma said. "She'll be here for Juneteenth. We got a lot of work to do to get ready."

Just what we needed—more work. But I didn't mind. At last there was something good to make up for all the bad things that were happening. Juneteenth and Susannah Jones.

Juneteenth—the nineteenth of June—was my favorite celebration, observing the date when the Negroes in Texas got word that they were free. President Lincoln signed the Emancipation Proclamation on January 1, 1863, but it wasn't until June 19, 1865—two and a half years later—that General Granger down in Galveston sent out the official Texas announcement. We always had a big to-do on that day, a church service and a picnic and a march and lots of speeches. White folks observed Memorial Day at the end of May to honor all the men who got killed in the War Between the States, but our people favored Juneteenth for our big time.

It was a good thing that Juneteenth fell on a Sunday that year. Everybody in Freedom had the day off and could celebrate the whole day without coming and going to and from their work, as often happened.

Aunt Susannah arrived the day before. I went with Poppa to the railroad depot to meet her train, wondering if I would recognize her. The Colored Only cars were jam-packed; lots of people were coming home to Freedom and other towns around Dillon to be with their families for Juneteenth. But I had no trouble picking her out of the crowd.

It wasn't only that she was so pretty and that her clothes looked better than almost everyone else's. It was that she carried herself like she was somebody special. Maybe that's what college did for you, I thought. She wore a navy blue traveling suit, nice as anything I ever saw Mrs. Bell dressed up in, and a hat, too—not the graduation cap in the picture, but a navy blue straw hat with a brim that dipped down on one side. The porter—who happened to be Lou Ann Hembry's poppa—set down two suitcases, both fine leather, on the platform beside her.

"That's her," Poppa said and stepped forward. He hugged her so hard her hat flew off, and he had to pick it up for her.

I hung back, suddenly shy, not able to think of a single word to say. Imagine having a fine colored lady like this in our family! I was excited but also a little worried: maybe she was used to something so much nicer than we had to offer. But she was holding out her hand, and I saw that she had on white gloves that weren't the least bit dirty from all the time she had spent on the train.

"You must be Rose Lee," she said, smiling.

I smiled back and shook her hand. That's when I noticed her green eyes. My aunt had green eyes!

About that time Poppa saw that he should have arranged for my uncle Walter to come with his taxicab. It was going to be a long walk to our house with those two big suitcases. Then he spied my friend Georgie Ellis's father with a taxi, and soon we had the two suitcases in the trunk. Poppa climbed in the front seat next to Mr. Ellis, and I was allowed to sit in back with my aunt. This was a rare event for me, and I hoped that Lou Ann Hembry or Bessie Morgan would see me riding in the backseat of a taxi with a lady in a big straw hat and be impressed.

Then came the next surprise. "I've written

to Mrs. Lipscomb and arranged to stay at the boardinghouse, Charles," Aunt Susannah said to my father. "No need to put you and Elvira and the children out."

I knew Momma would be shocked to hear this. In addition to her usual laundry work and all the preparations for Juneteenth, Momma had tuckered herself out cleaning our house, washing the windows and scrubbing the floors, hanging clean curtains, and shining the glass globes on all the coal-oil lamps. She had pinned freshly starched antimacassars on the backs and arms of her two good chairs in our sitting room that was also where Henry slept.

It had been decided that my two little sisters would stay with Grandfather Jim and Grandmother Lila, and Aunt Susannah would have the bed I usually shared with my sisters. I would make up a pallet on the floor. My sisters were excited at being allowed to stay with our grandparents although they were afraid they might miss something important if I got to stay with Aunt Susannah and they did not. Nevertheless, that's how we had worked it out. But now that was all suddenly changed.

The taxi took us to the Lipscombs' boardinghouse with the broad veranda and the second-floor balcony, nothing like the Bells' house but still very grand for Freedom. Poppa and Mr. Ellis got the suitcases out of the trunk and lugged them up the steps to the room that Mrs. Lipscomb was all in a flurry to show off. It was the best room, she said, located in the front of the house with a door opening out onto the balcony, and it had a parlor chair and a washstand. There was flowered wallpaper, which you did not see in Freedom except in Dr. Ragsdale's house, and a chenille counterpane on a bed the same size as the one I had to share with two sisters. I stroked the silky tufts of chenille that made a crisscross pattern and wished my aunt would invite me to stay with her in that pretty room.

"Thank you," said Aunt Susannah, taking off her hat and smoothing her hair, straight as any white lady's. "Now, Charles, if you'll just give me a little time to get settled in, to rest a bit and freshen up, I'll come by later to visit you and Elvira and the children."

I guessed Aunt Susannah didn't know Poppa had closed up his barbershop so he could go to the train to meet her, and Momma was still trying to finish up the week's laundry to be delivered to the white families on Oak Street, and pretty soon I had to run off and serve dinner at the Bells'. But Poppa said that would be fine, we'd be pleased to see her whenever she was ready, and reminded her how to find our house, one block over on Logan.

We said good-bye to Mrs. Lipscomb, who promised she'd see that Susannah had everything she needed. I followed Poppa down the stairs and out the front door.

"Well," Poppa said. "Looks like my little sister's turned into a fine lady."

"Uh huh," I said.

"Don't know if your momma's going to be glad or not that she's not staying in our house."

I guessed it would be a mixture of the two, and I was right. The only people who were really mad were my little sisters, who were now not going to stay with Grandmother and Grandfather. I was disappointed that I would not be sharing a room with this refined aunt of mine, but also relieved in a way.

No time now to think about that. I had to run all the way to Mrs. Bell's to get the table set for dinner. We weren't the only ones with visiting relatives: Mrs. Bell's brother and sister-in-law and their children had come up from Fort Worth to spend the night. I had ten people to serve.

———

SATURDAY, the day Aunt Susannah arrived, I helped Aunt Tillie fix the Sunday food for Mr. and Mrs. Bell and their family and friends. Aunt Tillie did not cook for them on Sundays, and I was not needed to serve, but we had to make sure there was plenty of food ready so Mrs. Bell and Catherine Jane could set it out whenever they wanted a meal. The visitors from Fort Worth meant we had to fix that much more.

Then after dinner Mr. and Mrs. Bell decided to invite their neighbors on Oak Street for a get-together that Saturday night, and Aunt Tillie and I had to stay late to serve and clean up. Aunt Tillie grumbled that Mrs. Bell always liked to give a party the night before she knew the Negroes were going to have a celebration, just out of meanness, so we'd be too tired to have a good time ourselves. But I didn't believe Mrs. Eunice Bell was mean. Just thoughtless.

All evening long I ran back and forth to the kitchen, carrying out silver trays with tiny sandwiches made with the crusts trimmed off the bread and cut in fancy shapes, and plates of cookies and little cakes arranged on white doilies. As soon as the trays were empty I took them out to Aunt Tillie, who kept fresh trays and platters filled and ready to exchange for the empty ones. On little side tables around the parlor and the sitting room were silver dishes, some with nuts and others with mints, that it was also my duty to keep filled. I had helped to polish all that silver, too.

On the dining-room table Aunt Tillie set the big ham she had baked and cut into thin slices, surrounded by plates of biscuits and little squares of corn bread and various kinds of pickles and relishes. A cut-glass punch bowl stood on the sideboard in the center of a ring of glass cups. There was no liquor in the punch, of course — it was lemonade with strawberries floating in it — because this was during Prohibition when liquor was illegal. I noticed that the men kept going upstairs to the smoker. Catherine Jane had told me once that she had found out her father kept bottles of gin and whiskey up there, so I knew the men were going up for what she called a "snort."

I still wore Cora's black shoes, which didn't fit, and my feet hurt. With all the busyness of the party and my hurting feet, I hardly had time to pay attention to who the guests were or what they were saying. I hoped I'd get a chance to talk to Catherine Jane and find out more about Miss Emily Firth, but there wasn't an opportunity for that. I did hear Mr. Tom Bell mention "our Fourth of July picnic and rally" to his neighbor, Mr. Tubbs. Then they disappeared, probably upstairs to the smoker.

It was very late when most of the people had gone and Mrs. Eunice Bell came to the kitchen to tell us we could go home. "Have a nice time at your get-together tomorrow," Mrs. Bell said, and Aunt Tillie and I bobbed our heads and said, "Yessum, thank you, ma'am," and hurried out of there as fast as our weary bones and aching feet could carry us.

"Your aunt Susannah Jones get here safe and sound?" Aunt Tillie asked. "I been too busy to ask."

"Yessum. She came this morning. She's staying at the Lipscombs'."

"At the boardinghouse? What she want to do that for?"

"Doesn't want to put us out," I explained.

"Huh," said Aunt Tillie.

"She's very nice," I added, not wanting Aunt Tillie to think my father's sister was snooty.

"I'm sure," Aunt Tillie said.

Then she started talking about Cora, and I was so tired I almost blurted out what Poppa said about Cora's husband, Ray, wanting to take Cora away to Oklahoma, but I managed to shut up in time.

"Sleep tight," Aunt Tillie said when we got to my house and she went on up the street.

Momma and Poppa were waiting for me. I had missed Aunt Susannah's visit, but I was too weary to care. I knew Momma would be waking me early to help with last-minute preparations and I wanted to have a good rest before the big day.

EIGHT

Juneteenth

WHEN I CAME into the kitchen the next morning, it looked like a whole flock of chickens had shed their feathers and roosted on our table. Momma whacked them up with her butcher knife, and it was my job to dip the pieces in egg and roll them in flour. Momma lowered each piece into the fat sizzling in a big iron kettle until soon we had three platters of fried chicken cooked and ready, enough to feed at least two dozen people, it looked like to me.

"Think, Rose Lee," Momma said, wiping her eyes on her sleeve. "This could be our last time to celebrate Juneteenth in this house."

But I was thinking about what we'd need to carry over to the church grove for the big picnic; I was too excited to think about such sad things as "our last time." Delicious food crowded every corner of our kitchen. Momma had been baking all the day before, sweet potato pies and pecan pies and a yellow cake with thick chocolate icing. It was almost like Mrs. Bell's kitchen the night before at her party, but ours was a different kind of eats, not so dainty and fine but hearty food that would stick to your ribs.

After a while Poppa strolled out of their bedroom in his undershirt, stretching and yawning. Then Nancy Lee and Lora Lee ran into the kitchen, rubbing sleep out of their eyes. They were no help at all but seemed always to be underfoot, good only for licking out the icing bowl and arguing over who got the spoon. Henry was still asleep on his cot in the sitting room, and Momma made us tiptoe around and whisper until he woke up on his own. Even if he had been willing, Momma would not have asked Henry for help.

Because it was Sunday and a special occasion, too, Momma fried up pan sausage and eggs for our breakfast and made gravy to pour over the grits, and there were hot buttermilk biscuits and Grandmother Lila's grape preserve. Then it was time to dress up in our good clothes. Even Henry got up and ready, but he looked sour and miserable, as if he hadn't had a good night's sleep or a decent meal in days.

I put on my best dress that had once belonged to Catherine Jane, yellow organdy with a dropped waist and sawtooth hem, and my good white shoes that pinched. Seems all my shoes were either too big or too small.

When I was ready, I was sent to the boardinghouse to fetch Aunt Susannah, so she could walk to church with our family. I found her sitting in a rocking chair on the front porch of Mrs. Lipscomb's, fanning herself with a white lace hankie. She stood up when I appeared, and I saw that she was wearing a red dress — flame red, red as the four-o'clocks in the Garden of Eden — with a deep ruffle around the neck and the hem. She wore a little red hat that came down over her ears, and she carried an umbrella the same color, which seemed like a good idea, because it did sometimes rain late in the day.

"Good morning, Rose Lee!" she called out and hurried down the steps to meet me. Red shoes, too, with tall, spindly heels. "How nice you look today!" She opened the red umbrella — it had a ruffle on it, too — and propped it on her shoulder so that it cast a shadow, and I understood that it was not for keeping off rain but sun. That's when I noticed the ring, gold with a big green stone, green like her eyes, and a lot of little tiny diamonds around it. She saw me staring. "You like my parasol?"

It wasn't the parasol I was staring at. "Yessum."

We stepped into the dirt streets of Freedomtown. You had to be very careful where you put your feet so as not to spoil your shoes. But Aunt Susannah seemed not at all worried about her beautiful red shoes. She was too busy looking around, asking questions and admiring all she saw. "I haven't been here for years," she said. "Since the summer I finished high school. You were just a little bit of a thing. I hope you'll agree to be my guide."

"Yessum."

I began to look at Freedom as it must have appeared to Aunt Susannah's eyes, everything neat and tidy. "Is it like this in St. Louis?" I asked, and that made her laugh.

"Not at all," she said. "That's a different world. But someday you'll come there and see for yourself."

Had I heard her right? This day was getting better every minute.

Naturally I made sure to take her by Grandfather Jim's for a look at the Garden of Eden. His precious white lilac bush had finished blooming, but morning glories covered the fence and orange day lilies and red zinnias and pink and blue periwinkles and lavender and white petunias and I don't know what all, every color you could think of, bloomed in beds edged with bricks. Wild honeysuckle covered every corner of the yard where nothing else grew and filled the morning air with its sweet scent.

"Oh, Rose Lee!" Aunt Susannah said, her amazing green eyes shining with delight. "I had forgotten how beautiful it is! Your grandfather is an absolute genius!"

While we were looking, the big bell started ringing at Forgiveness Baptist Church, calling us to services. Every Sunday that bell rang for something — Sunday School, which had been suspended today because it was a special occasion, and church, and afternoon service, and evening prayer meeting. You could hear that big bell ringing in every house in Freedom.

I urged Aunt Susannah gently away from Grandfather's toward my own house. I knew not to take her through Poppa's barbershop where the cracked yellow blinds had been pulled down to let customers know it was closed, but led her directly into Momma's spotless kitchen by way of the back door, like family. Company was to come in through the sitting room, and the look on Momma's face told me better than words that I had made a mistake. Aunt Susannah was still definitely company.

They were all waiting for us. My little sisters had bows tied in their braids that matched their party dresses. Poppa had on his black suit, shiny from Momma's pressing, and a shirt with a starched collar. Momma wore her best white dress with two rows of polished black buttons marching down the front. Henry didn't own a real suit, but he'd put on a pair of clean trousers and a perfectly ironed shirt and one of Poppa's neckties. He looked very handsome, and I was certain that Aunt Susannah would notice and approve.

One thing is sure, Henry and everybody else noticed *her* — the red dress, red shoes, red parasol. "My," said Momma. "That is a *striking* outfit, Susannah." And I nearly died of embarrassment, because I knew Momma and I knew her tone of voice and choice of words meant she didn't think much of Aunt Susannah's clothes.

But all Aunt Susannah said was, "It's cheerful. And from what you told me last night, we could all use some cheering up around here."

"Takes more than a red dress," Henry said, and Momma gave him a sharp look.

"But it's a start, Henry," Aunt Susannah replied.

"Time to go," said Poppa without even checking his watch. The bell was still ringing.

We walked to Forgiveness Baptist together, two by two except Henry, who came last, a little apart from us. Others of our neighbors stepped out of their houses, either staring at us openly (staring at Aunt Susannah, to be exact) or staring but pretending not to, nodding greetings to my parents, speaking about the weather — rain was a possibility; there were some purplish thunderheads in the distance — and joined the procession of people on their way to church, some to Forgiveness and others to Mt. Olive African Methodist Episcopal over on Roberts Street. AME, we called it.

We were early enough to be sure of getting good seats and filed into a pew toward the front, Momma first, then my sisters and me, followed by Aunt Susannah, leaving Poppa on the end of the pew. I noticed Henry wasn't with us anymore; stopped to speak to his friends, I guessed. I kept cutting my eyes over to my aunt, to see if she knew that nobody had ever worn such a bright red dress to church. But she looked perfectly easy. Then I tried to look around to see how people were noticing *her*, like Bessie Morgan and her folks, but Momma sent me a "behave yourself" message with her eyebrows, and I turned to face straight ahead.

When the church was filled, packed so tight it seemed there was not room for one more person to squeeze onto the hard benches, Pastor Mobley walked down the aisle dressed all in white — white suit, white shirt, white necktie, and gleaming white shoes — and announced the first hymn, even though we all knew what it was going to be: "The Battle Hymn of the Republic." We didn't have a piano at Forgiveness (they did over at Mt. Olive), but we didn't need one. Everybody knew that hymn, not only the melody and the harmony, but all the words of all the verses, and we sang out at the top of our voices, especially on the chorus:

> *Glory, glory, hallelujah!*
> *Glory, glory, hallelujah!*

It stirred us all. I noticed that Aunt Susannah standing right beside me in her flame red dress loved to sing, too, and that pleased me.

Then Pastor Mobley led some prayers, and the choir, which included my aunt Tillie, sang some hymns, starting off with "Swing Low, Sweet Chariot." You would never have known, working alongside Aunt Tillie in Mrs. Bell's kitchen, listening to her complain about the way I was serving the dishes or clearing them away, that she had such a beautiful voice, rich as sorghum molasses.

Next they sang "Steal Away," and Aunt Tillie had the solo: "My Lord calls me, He calls me by the thunder," and just then there was a great clap of thunder outside, which made everyone gasp.

The preacher asked Mr. Morgan, Bessie's father, to step forward and read the Emancipation Proclamation, the words of President Abraham Lincoln. Mr. Morgan was an elder in the church and got to do it every year. Next Mr. Lipscomb read General Granger's Proclamation: "The people of Texas are informed that in accordance with a proclamation from the Executive of the United States all slaves are free. Signed, G. Granger, Major General, Commanding Galveston, Texas, June nineteenth, 1865."

When he said those words everybody shouted "Amen!" and it resounded through our plain wooden church. I felt happiness surging up inside me.

Then we all settled down to listen to Pastor Mobley's sermon. "Brothers and sisters," he began, "the Lord is putting us to the test. Let us listen to the words of Job." He opened his worn black Bible to a place marked with a purple ribbon and read: "How long will ye vex my soul, and break me in pieces with words?" Then he closed the Book and spoke to us about what was happening to Freedom, and how it had come to pass that we could be asked to give up our homes, our community, to bow to the will of those who would "break us in pieces."

Deep mutterings of "Amen" and "Yes, yes" swept through the packed church like a sigh. It was hot and getting hotter. A lazy fly buzzed around. Cardboard fans with pictures of Jesus in a garden fluttered in the women's hands. My little sisters fidgeted and whispered until Momma shushed them. The tiredness began to well up where the happiness had been, and my mind started to drift·away. The pastor's voice was soothing, and I closed my eyes for just a second.

"But remember these words: We are commanded to love one another. We are commanded to forgive one another. It may come to pass that we will have to go forth and rebuild, as many have done before us. But we will do it in humility, trusting in God's abiding love for us."

"Amen," the people said. "Yes, Lord."

"No!" someone shouted from the back of the church. My eyes flew open and my head snapped up, and we all turned to see who had spoken. I saw my brother Henry standing in the back of the church, a head taller than the other men. Momma let out a little cry, and Henry said again, "No!" and came down the aisle in long strides. "We can't let this happen!" he said, his voice filling the church.

Henry reached the front of the church and stepped in front of Pastor Mobley, who reached out a hand to protest and then drew it back. "We can't let the white man take away our homes to build his parks, to protect his women from the filthy presence of a colored child!" Henry said. "We must say no to anyone who tries to take away from us what is ours. We must say no in a way the white man understands, so that he can make no mistake about it!" The anger in his voice rang out, stunning everyone in silence. "We have a choice, brothers and sisters. We stand and fight, or we leave, all of us together."

Henry began to pace back and forth in front of the church. His dark face glistened with sweat, and his eyes glittered. No one moved. No one dared to breathe. I heard Momma begin to weep softly. Aunt Susannah's white linen hankie hung limp in her hand like a little flag while she gazed up at my brother.

"What do you think would happen," Henry demanded, "if there were no niggers in Dillon? What do you think would happen to the white people if every single one of us—every man, woman, and child—left this place, went away and left it to them? Left it to them to cook their own food, wash their own clothes, tend their own gardens, care for their own children?"

His voice had risen, but now it dropped to just above a whisper. I leaned forward, so as not to miss a word he said. "What do you think would happen, brothers and sisters, if we were to leave it all to them, and go to the Promised Land? The Promised Land! I don't mean St. Louis, where my aunt has just come from. I don't mean Chicago. I don't mean any place in this white man's country. Let him have all of it!

"No," he said, and you could feel the fever pounding in him, the excitement growing in the people watching him breathlessly. His clean white shirt was damp. "No! I mean Africa, brothers and sisters! Where we can join with other black brothers and sisters! Africa calls us! It's time! Leave this stinking white man's world to the white man! Africa is ours! Who will join me? Because I'm going to Liberia! Anyone else feels like I do, come forward now and stand by me."

Murmurs rippled through the congregation. Momma's quiet tears blossomed into sobs. Then my father in his shiny black suit rose and made his way resolutely to the front of the church. Henry watched him coming. Poppa was a tall man, but Henry was taller, heavier.

"I understand you, son," Poppa said so quietly that we all had to strain to hear. "But you must understand us, too. This family is staying in Dillon, one way or another. Now go sit down, Henry, and let Pastor Mobley get on with the service."

For a time Henry stood firm, his hands clenched into huge fists, his chest rising and falling. And then his hands fell open at his sides, he nodded once to my father, brushed past him, and walked down the aisle and out of the church. Poppa stood with his head bowed. You could hear everyone let out the breath they had been holding, like the wind in the trees. Pastor Mobley stepped forward again and cleared his throat. "We have heard Brother Henry's opinion," he said. "Let us all rise and join our voices in our final hymn."

This was the part I always liked best, not just because it was at the end: the song we call the Negro National Anthem, "Lift Every Voice and Sing," composed by James Weldon Johnson and his brother, John Rosamond Johnson. The ladies of the choir, led by my aunt Tillie, took high notes that soared like birds above the melody sung by the congregation.

We were so deeply stirred by our singing that the shock of Henry's sudden appearance was lessened. Of course I was wondering all this time what our aunt must be thinking of my hot-headed brother. I tried another look at Aunt Susannah, standing tall and proud beside me. Tears shone in her eyes.

One more prayer, the benediction, and it was over. Everyone poured out of the stifling church and into the shady grove where the men had set up makeshift tables and benches. The thunderclouds had passed away and the sky was clear and bright. I could see the excitement on all the faces, the questions when they looked our way. I could see, too, that Momma was upset and Poppa seemed far away and thoughtful. I was part proud of Henry for standing up and speaking out so boldly and also part scared for what he had said, and those parts fought with each other. Maybe other folks were fighting those same battles in their heads, but for the time being no one said a word about Henry.

NINE

Marchers

WE HAD NOT yet started to unpack the food when the service ended down at Mt. Olive. Their people came marching up Roberts Street, carrying a banner with the name of their church on it, and they were singing. They were coming to join us, so that everybody in Freedom could be together for Juneteenth. We were providing the picnic for those folks as well as for ourselves. Next year it would be their turn, and we'd go to the AME church to share their spread. That's how it had been in the past, getting together and sharing, taking turns. But then it came to me that maybe Momma was right, and Henry, too—there might not *be* a next year for Freedomtown, at least not here, in this place.

When we heard "Lift Every Voice and Sing," we started over to greet them, to march around Freedom together as we did every year. One of the men of the church carried our banner, which my Grandmother Lila had made a long time ago, before I was even born.

"May I walk with you, Rose Lee?" Aunt Susannah asked, her red parasol already open.

"Yessum," I said, pleased as could be.

First we all marched down Logan Street, past our house and the Garden of Eden, then we cut over at Mayhew to Roberts, all nice and shady with the big old oaks and pecans and hackberry trees leafed out, and then back on to Brown. I pointed out my schoolhouse, which had four rooms, two up and two down, and the Sun-Up Café where Poppa's Masonic Lodge held its meetings on the second floor. "Momma's not in Eastern Star," I told Aunt Susannah. "Grandmother Lila wanted her to belong to the Household of Ruth, same as she does." The Household of Ruth was an organization of ladies who met in each other's homes and were pledged to take care of each other in time of need. The Household of Ruth would hear plenty about my brother Henry, I was sure, and might even have a good deal to say about my aunt Susannah and her flame red dress.

We marched on, Aunt Tillie's powerful voice ringing out above everybody's. "That's the Knights of Pythias Hall," I said, pointing out a plain wooden building on Brown Street. "They have dances there, but I'm not old enough to go. And there are picture shows there, too, when the traveling shows come through town. Colored folks aren't allowed to go to the picture shows over on the square," I said. "But I guess you know that."

"Yes, Rose Lee," she said. "I know. Jim Crow is one of the reasons I left the South."

We turned up Edwards Street. I thought we were going to walk once around Freedom and back to the church, like always, but the leaders up front with the banners changed direction and turned west, out of Freedom. I don't know whose idea it was, it just seemed to happen, but we kept on marching and folks kept on singing, all the way over to the courthouse square.

Somebody must have heard us coming and gotten the sheriff, because when we reached the courthouse several white men on horseback appeared at each corner of the square. They stared at us, their faces hard and blank as stone, their horses nickering and pawing the ground. We paid no attention to them but kept on singing and marching, circling once around the square, past the statue of the Confederate soldier that some of the white ladies had raised money to put up a couple of years earlier. Men, women, and children sang and marched. Aunt Susannah gripped my hand the whole time, her head held high, her red parasol bobbing. Then we headed back to Freedom and the church grove where some of the old people who didn't feel up to parading had stayed behind to keep an eye on our picnic baskets. Grandmother Lila was one who waited for us, hands on her hips, as though she had been expecting some kind of trouble.

She had laid some of her old quilts over rough wooden boards and then spread two of her best embroidered tablecloths on top of them so it looked almost as fine as Mrs. Bell's dinner table. When we got back from our march, Grandmother and Momma and Aunt Tillie and my aunts Flora and Vinnie began putting out the food.

We called to some folks from Mt. Olive, including Lou Ann Hembry and her poppa and momma and brothers, and they came to eat with us. Aunt Flora's girl, Grace, and her beau, Lester Sledge, carried over more benches. I thought Lester was nice, but Aunt Flora wasn't altogether happy about him because she hoped

Grace would win a music scholarship somewhere for her piano playing, and all Grace wanted to do was get married. Counting all the cousins, including Lester, there were twenty-six people crowded around our spread. Bessie Morgan was supposed to be with her folks, but soon enough she came over to be with us.

The biggest baskets were filled with our platters of fried chicken, and there were several more baskets with all the things you'd expect to find at a Freedom picnic: various pickled vegetables, like okra and beets, and golden loaves of bread and jars of fruit jam to spread on the thick slices Momma cut for us and a lump of butter wrapped in wet canvas to keep it from melting away in the heat. From other baskets came cakes and pies and fruit cobblers. Grandfather brought three great big watermelons from his garden, and Mr. Webster, the owner of the Sun-Up Café, supplied red soda pop for everyone, as much as you wanted. It turned out, as it always did, there was more than enough for everybody.

I liked having Bessie and Lou Ann there with me, but Bessie, as always, was full of questions. "Are y'all going to Africa, Rose Lee?" she asked as we were going to get another red soda out of the washtub where a block of ice kept them cool.

"No," I said. "We're not. Poppa says we're not going anywhere."

"My poppa says we're going to move someplace, but it's sure not going to be Africa. He says a mortician is always able to find a good place to live." (Bessie was always careful to say "mortician" instead of "undertaker.")

"You'd go away from here?" Lou Ann asked.

"Poppa wants to, but Momma doesn't," Bessie said. "She says we got too many kin here."

"Same in my family," Lou Ann said. I guess everybody was confused.

Then Bessie changed the subject. "I love your aunt's red parasol," she said to me. "I thought you said she was a schoolteacher."

"She is."

"Schoolteachers don't dress like that. I saw her ring, too. I think it's an emerald."

"They dress that way in St. Louis," I assured her, wondering if that was true.

"Do you think she'd let me carry her parasol for a while?"

"I don't know," I said. "Let's ask."

But before we got the chance to ask, Aunt Susannah suddenly murmured "Excuse me," and walked away from our table. We watched her go up to Pastor Mobley and speak to him, but we couldn't make out what she said. They made quite a sight: him in his white suit, her in her red dress.

Pastor Mobley listened to her, nodding. Then in his booming voice that carried so well he said, "I am very happy now to introduce a special guest, Miss Susannah Jones of St. Louis, Missouri, who is visiting her brother, Charles Jefferson, and his family. Sister Susannah would like to address a few words to us on this occasion. Kindly give her your attention."

This was unusual on two counts: she was a woman, and the women in our community left most of the public speaking to the men, and also she was a stranger to Freedom. Everyone clapped politely, but you could almost hear the question marks in that applause. Then Pastor Mobley helped her climb up on a bench, so that she could be seen and heard, and stepped aside. I saw Momma's mouth drop open, and she shot Poppa a disapproving look.

"I'm honored to be here among you today," she said, not sounding the least bit nervous, "grateful to my brother Charles and my sister-in-law Elvira and their children." Here she smiled directly at me, and Bessie poked me. "I wish to express to all of you my heartfelt support at this difficult time in the life of your community. This morning some of us heard Pastor Mobley urge you to have humility, to trust in God's love. Some of us also heard a young man of this community, my brother's son, urge you to make a hard choice: to stand and fight, or to leave this place to the white man and to return to Africa. And we heard my brother speak of his determination to stay in Dillon, one way or another."

I looked at my momma, and she seemed to be embarrassed almost to death that someone else in the family was standing up in front of everybody, making a speech, "calling attention," as Momma put it. She glared at Henry as if all of this was his fault. But everybody else was waiting to hear what Aunt Susannah would say next.

"I know these are not easy decisions to make. Some may choose to stay, no matter under what conditions. Some may choose to resist, regardless of the risk. And some may choose to leave, for another town, or another continent. My words to you are this: Trust the Lord and talk about it among yourselves. Trusting God is one thing, but you must also trust one another. And don't be afraid.

'Ye fearful saints fresh courage take,
The clouds ye so much dread

Are big with mercy, and shall break
In blessings on your head.'

From a poem by English poet William Cowper. Thank you."

She stepped down from the bench, resting her hand lightly on Pastor Mobley's elbow for balance. Everyone clapped again, enthusiastically this time, and a few people called out "Amen!" A third unusual thing was that we weren't used to such short speeches.

Aunt Susannah's speech seemed to change everything. Everybody had been pretending, I guess, that Henry had not suddenly appeared in Forgiveness Baptist a few hours ago and made his speech, urging us to move to Africa if we weren't going to fight back. And I got the idea that everybody worried and everybody whispered, but nobody really *discussed* anything. If there were sixty families in Freedom, then there must have been sixty different ideas — or maybe a hundred and twenty, if husbands and wives disagreed as much as Momma and Poppa did, and you added in the sons and daughters like Henry who had different ideas altogether and was getting into discussions — Momma called them arguments — with anybody who would listen.

The afternoon wore on, and now everybody

was talking about what they were going to do. The little kids got restless with all the adult conversation and ran around shouting, and some of them fell asleep. Lou Ann and Bessie clustered shyly around Aunt Susannah, asking her questions about St. Louis. Then Bessie and Lou Ann wanted me to go for a walk with them, borrowing the red parasol, but I declined. I wanted to stay and hear what folks were saying.

Most people thought Henry was wrong. They started to argue about Marcus Garvey and his "back to Africa" movement, and Henry pulled out a copy of a newspaper that Mr. Garvey published called *Negro World*. The paper was almost worn out from reading. Henry said he knew of a few families from Grover Point, a little town up north of Dillon toward the Oklahoma border, who sailed from Galveston in 1916, bound for Liberia. Henry appeared to worship this Mr. Garvey, who was an important man in Harlem and would be coming to Dallas before long to address the chapter of the UNIA Henry had joined. Henry was determined to learn as much as he could from him. Poppa called Marcus Garvey a rabble-rouser, which Henry didn't like at all. But before the afternoon was over, Henry had convinced a couple of other young men — including Lester Sledge — to come to the meeting.

Late in the afternoon we began to pack up the leftovers, Momma urging everyone to take a little something home with them, since we'd never be able to eat it all ourselves. I said I'd walk with Aunt Susannah to the Lipscombs' boardinghouse. Before I had gone half a block I took off my shoes and carried them. I could savor this time better if my feet didn't hurt.

"I worry about your brother," Aunt Susannah said. "He could place himself in a lot of danger."

"Yessum."

"I hope he's careful how he speaks out."

"Yessum," I said, but I knew Henry wasn't careful.

Then we said good-bye, and Aunt Susannah went on into Mrs. Lipscomb's and I ran home, enjoying the feel of the damp earth on my bare feet.

DURING THE NIGHT after the time that everyone was generally asleep, I awoke to a sound I could not identify. It was hot in the little bedroom, and my sticky, sweaty little sisters sighed and turned over in their sleep. I crept out of the bed we all three slept in and went out to see what was going on.

My parents were not in their room. Still in

my ragged nightdress I pushed past the heavy green curtain that separated the barbershop from the rest of the house. They were standing at the window, taking turns peeping out through a narrow slit in the drawn shade. I could sense their fear.

"What is it?" I whispered.

"Go back to bed, Rose Lee," Momma said in a croaky voice. That voice and the look on her face told me something terrible was happening. But I didn't move, whether from stubbornness or fear, I don't know. "Go," she repeated.

Poppa turned from the window and reached out for me. I rushed into his arms. "It's the Klan," he said, holding me tight. "They're marching." With his free hand he adjusted the shade a bit so I could see.

It was a terrifying sight: an endless procession of figures, all dressed in long white robes and tall, pointed hoods that completely covered their faces, with only holes cut for the eyes. The hooded figures kept coming and coming, hundreds of them it seemed, marching past our house. No speaking, no shouting, no singing — no sound at all but the *tramp, tramp, tramp* of their feet. Holding on to each other, we watched them pass.

"Where are they going, Poppa?"

"I don't know. We have to wait and see."

"But why are they here?" I asked, trying to keep my voice steady. "What do they want?" But I didn't have to ask. I knew.

"They want Freedomtown," Poppa said. "They want to make sure we're too scared to argue with them."

When the last of the hooded men had passed, Poppa said, "Now Rose Lee, I'm going outside for a better look. You and your momma stay right here."

We watched him creep out of the house, bent low behind our fence. A moment later, heedless of the danger, Momma rushed out to join him, waving a warning finger at me to stay behind. I ran after her, scared, but too scared not to.

The Klan marchers reached our church. They crowded the grove where we had our picnic. From our hiding place I could see one of them dig a hole in the ground with a shovel. Then two more planted a big wooden cross in the hole, while the man with the shovel packed dirt around it. Someone doused the cross with liquid from a can. Someone else lit a match and jumped back. Flames leaped up, and the cross began to burn like a torch.

"Remember this, niggers!" a hooded man shouted. And then they all began to yell, and I put my hands over my ears to shut it out. While the flames swallowed up the wooden cross, the men moved away, melting into the darkness, leaving the cross to burn in the church grove. We could tell by the sound of their voices, still yelling, that they were on their way to the courthouse square.

"I don't think they'll come back tonight," my father said, straightening up.

"But they'll be back sometime," my mother said grimly.

Gradually, a few at a time, we saw our neighbors come out of hiding places, from behind fences and bushes and porches, and gather in the street. Aunt Tillie, who lived across the street from the church, appeared in a pink, flowered wrapper, tears rolling down her cheeks. Slowly we walked toward Forgiveness Church, our eyes fixed on the burning cross. No one spoke. We stood in silence, too numbed to say anything, until the cross had burned to red-glowing cinders, a charred spot on the ground.

Suddenly I remembered Henry. Where was he? Surely he would not have slept through this. I tugged Momma's sleeve. "I'm going back inside, Momma," I said and pretended to yawn, although I was anything but sleepy.

"See that your sisters are all right, will you, Rose Lee?"

I said I would, but truthfully I had forgotten about them. It was Henry I was worried about.

I ran back down our street and let myself into the house through the kitchen. Then I stole through the sitting room, close to the cot that was my brother's bed. The cot was empty, his quilt not even disturbed.

With a heavy heart I crept into my own bed in the next room, making a space for myself next to my sisters, who had sprawled into my side of our bed while I was gone. I lay still, listening. After what seemed like a long while, I heard Momma and Poppa come in, the door close, the springs sing as they climbed into their bed on the other side of the wall, the low undertones of their voices. For the rest of the night I tossed restlessly, flinging myself this way and that, trying to find a spot that would give me rest.

In my memory, Juneteenth 1921 was the last good day for Freedomtown, all of us together in one place. It seemed fitting that the day had ended with a flaming cross in the church grove. It was a sight I'd never forget.

TEN

More Lessons

HENRY TURNED UP safe the next day, but he would not talk about where he had been. And from then on he told us little of his doings or his whereabouts. My brother would come home from the brickyard, sweaty and coated with fine yellow dust. Then he would bathe, dress, eat whatever Momma set in front of him, and go right out again. Sometimes he slept on his cot in the sitting room, but often he did not. We suspected he was with Garvey people some-place, making plans.

"He's a grown man. Twenty-one years old,"

Poppa reminded Momma when she fretted. "He fought in France."

"I know. I know."

But no matter how grown they were, Momma worried a lot about her children. She had already lost two of us, a baby to diphtheria before I was born and my brother Jack when the influenza was so bad in 1918 and so many died that our school closed down and we were even afraid to go to church. Momma had sent for the doctor but he couldn't help, and Jack died at the age of sixteen. Henry was already in the army, fighting on the other side of the ocean. It was after Henry came home that he started getting wild, claiming the country owed colored boys something for fighting in their war.

After Juneteenth there were only sixteen days until the bond issue would be voted on. Every day I counted the days left until July fifth on the calendar in Poppa's barbershop. Two weeks plus two days. It seemed that everyone in Freedom knew how the vote was going to turn out, but we still didn't know what we were going to do. The men gathered 'most every night in Poppa's barbershop, talking and discussing and sometimes arguing until very late, going over and over the same thing.

"They'll have to haul me away," Grandfather said, but a minute later he seemed to change his mind. "No use, no use," he said with a sigh. "I'm just an old man." Back and forth he went.

Mr. Ross, the supervisor of all the janitors at the Academy, argued it was useless to fight. "If the city council and the white property owners decide to move us off our land, then that's what's going to happen," he said. "Best thing is to try to get them to give us a fair price for our property so we can start over somewhere else."

"Yes, but where? That's the question."

"Mayor Dixon says we can go out by The Flats," said Mr. Alexander, who held a job as a foreman at the brickyard, which was owned by Mayor Dixon. Poppa said Mr. Alexander often took up for the white bosses. Too often. "Mayor Dixon says we can have all the land we want out there," Mr. Alexander said, "and they'll help us move. Lend us mules to pick up our houses and tote 'em right out there, no cost to us."

"Out there by the cesspool? Who wants to live out there, tell me that?" Mr. Webster demanded.

"Not a soul lives out there now," Mr. Morgan said. "It's just land nobody wants."

I knew the place they meant — a smelly old cow pasture on the far side of the railroad tracks without so much as a tree. But if not there, then where? No one knew. I sat and listened to them talk, and Momma didn't seem to care anymore if I did. I guess she thought I'd heard so much bad language since our troubles started that it wouldn't matter anymore. And the men made no objection to me being there.

A lot depended, I heard the men say, on how much the city council was willing to pay us for our property. If they paid what the men felt it was actually worth, then maybe they could set themselves up again in some other part of Dillon, as long as it wasn't The Flats.

"Don't be foolish," Mr. Lipscomb said. "White folks don't think our houses are worth anything, and that's what they're going to pay us — nothing. You'll see."

Before the vote was taken, the men decided to send a letter of protest to the city council. That was Poppa's idea. They realized that they couldn't change the way the vote would turn out, but they could insist on fair treatment, even though Mr. Lipscomb kept saying we'd never get it. Pastor Mobley was chosen to sit down and put their suggestions into the proper formal language. I was in the barbershop a few nights later when the preacher read out what he had written: "We, as citizens, are making an earnest appeal that you give compensation that all property is worth. We will also be able to make permanent location after settlement is made. Hoping this report will meet your approval," and so on. After a good deal more debate, the men signed. Except Mr. Lipscomb.

While the men debated in Poppa's barbershop, the women discussed it in their own way, coming by to visit with Momma, to talk about the Fourth of July fish fry, to gossip about Aunt Susannah (that's how I found out—by eavesdropping—that her engagement to a businessman in St. Louis had been broken and that the real reason she had come to visit us was to "gather herself," as Momma put it).

It was a sad day when the first people in Freedom made up their minds to move away: Mr. Watson, who had a shoe-repair shop, decided to give it up and go live with a daughter in Nebraska. His wife, Ella, confided the news to the Household of Ruth. All the ladies broke down and cried that night, Momma said, Ella Watson most of all. Others, like Bessie Morgan's folks, talked about leaving, but Mr. and Mrs. Watson had already started to pack.

In the days that followed we tried to go on with our lives the way they were before, but our nerves were stretched tight as banjo strings, waiting for a reply from Mayor Dixon and the city council, and still trying to think what to do.

ON THE Friday after Juneteenth I came home from Mrs. Bell's and found Aunt Susannah ironing in our kitchen.

"Elvie's at a Household of Ruth meeting," she said, "and I'm trying to help her out. They're planning a fish fry *and* a pie sale, did you know that?"

"Yessum," I said, getting out the pork chop Momma had put aside for me. "They always do that on the Fourth. You'll like it. It's fun."

"Well then, we'll have to go together."

Aunt Susannah was ironing linen napkins. I recognized Mrs. Bell's, with the embroidery in the corner. The trick was to iron them while they were still wet, but Aunt Susannah didn't seem to know that trick. It didn't look to me like she had ever done much ironing. Momma wasn't going to be happy with this, I knew, and Mrs. Bell wouldn't be happy *at all*.

"I could help you with that," I said, although I hated ironing more than almost anything.

"They don't look very good, do they?" She sighed. "Maybe you could just show me how to do it the right way. Your mother took it for granted I know how, and I didn't want to tell

117

her how much about keeping house this school-teacher doesn't know."

I showed her then how to lay a towel on the ironing board and spread out the damp napkin with the embroidered part face down and go over it until it was ironed completely dry and stiff, and she told me about how she taught English in a high school.

"Who's your favorite poet, Rose Lee?" she asked.

"Whoever wrote *A Child's Garden of Verses*," I said, remembering Catherine Jane's book.

"Robert Louis Stevenson," she said. "Mine's Lord Byron." Then she began to recite for me in a voice every bit as beautiful as Aunt Tillie's:

> *"She walks in beauty, like the night*
> *Of cloudless climes and starry skies . . .*

"You like to read poetry, Rose Lee?"

"I haven't read much, tell the truth, except Mr. Stevenson's."

"So what do you like to do, Rose Lee? Do you have plans for your life?"

Nobody had ever asked me anything like that, and I was taken aback by her question. "I like to draw," I said after a bit, "but so far I don't have a plan."

"Maybe drawing is your plan. Will you show me some of your pictures?"

"Yes," I said, feeling pleased.

We wrestled to get a great big tablecloth folded just right. "How long you going to stay here?" I asked. Poppa had said she was spending some time with us, but I didn't know if that was a week or a month, and she hadn't said.

"Here's the truth," Aunt Susannah said, testing the iron with her finger. "I was engaged to be married. We were planning a fine wedding—I even ordered a white satin gown with a train flowing out in back and a white veil trimmed with lace. And he gave me this ring." She held up her hand, where the beautiful green stone shone brightly. "But that ended, just like that." She snapped her fingers and the ring glittered.

"How come?" I asked, glad Momma was not around to shush me and say it was none of my business.

"I decided it would be a serious mistake. John's a nice man, but it wouldn't have worked. Much better to stay friends."

Then she set down the iron and opened her purse—a yellow one that day, to match her yellow dress—and showed me a picture of the man she had decided not to marry, even after the gown had been ordered and the hall reserved for a big party. I squinted at the photograph of a smiling, light-skinned man with a thin mustache, handsome as any movie star.

"Looks almost white," I said.

She laughed. "That's because he *is* white."

I stared at her. "But colored girls are not allowed to marry a white man," I said. "It's against the law."

"Against the law in Texas," she said, "but not up North. In this case, though, his family had something to say about it. Told him he wouldn't get a dime of their money when they died if he married me, and he said he was going to go ahead and do it anyway, no matter what they said, and I told him no, that's not right, either, and I handed back his ring. But he said no, keep it, 'as a memento.' That's when I wrote to your momma and poppa and said I wanted to come down here for a visit. After that experience, I thought it was a good idea for me to spend some time with kinfolk."

She put the photograph back in her purse, and I thought she didn't look as easy as she tried to sound and it must have hurt her bad to have to tell that handsome white man she wasn't going to marry him after all.

Then I asked her another question that had been troubling me ever since she arrived in

Freedom. "How come you got green eyes?" I asked her. "Poppa doesn't."

"Your poppa and I have the same momma but different poppas," she said. "My poppa's daddy was a white man. Your poppa's was Indian, if I remember rightly."

"Seminole," I said. "How come it was all right for your granddaddy to be white but it's not all right for you to marry a white man?"

"Didn't say my granddaddy was *married* to my grandma, now did I, Rose Lee?"

"No, ma'am." We flipped the tablecloth over so she could get at the other side. It wasn't as good as when Momma did it, but I figured it was good enough.

That was the first of many talks I was to have with Aunt Susannah, talks I'm sure my momma would not have approved of. I was learning about the world, according to Aunt Susannah. *Too much,* Momma would have said.

MEANWHILE Henry was saying more and more how white folks needed to learn a lesson about how much they needed Negroes to do their work for them. "Only way they going to learn what it's going to cost them to turn us out of our homes," Henry said, "is if we *show* them."

"What you mean by that, Henry?" Poppa asked. "How you intend to show them?"

"Stop doing their work. Refuse, for just one day, to do anything for them. Let them do it themselves."

"You crazy, boy? Pull a stunt like that and it's likely the last work you get from anybody in Dillon!"

"Not if we all do it, Poppa," Henry said earnestly. "Not if every single one of us make up our minds to cooperate and do it at the same time. I'm thinking next Monday."

"Monday? Fourth of July?"

"Yes. That's the day the white folks all have their big picnic and barbecue out at the fairgrounds. And who goes out and digs the barbecue pit and builds the fire and tends the meat? We do. Who bakes all the cakes and pies and goes along to make sure everything goes right? Same answer. It's their holiday, all right, but Fourth of July is supposed to be Independence Day for us, too, only we always have to work. I bet Momma doesn't have any day off from her washtubs and clotheslines and ironing boards!"

"Well now," Poppa said.

Suddenly Henry turned to me. "What about you, Rose Lee? You supposed to be over at Mr. and Mrs. Bell's house bright and early, fix 'em their breakfast, fix 'em their lunch, get their picnic ready for the barbecue?"

"Not breakfast," I said, not wanting to get into this plan of Henry's. "I don't have to help with breakfast."

"But Aunt Tillie does, doesn't she?"

"Yes."

"Well then. Suppose Aunt Tillie doesn't go to Mrs. Bell's on Monday, and neither do you. What do you think would happen then?"

"I don't know," I said, getting a little scared.

"Teach 'em a lesson, wouldn't it?"

"Maybe so."

"Henry, leave her alone. She's only a child," Poppa said, and while I was glad not to have Henry talking to me like that, I didn't like being called a child.

I thought and thought about it. I wondered if he'd tell Aunt Tillie she shouldn't work on the Fourth of July, and I wondered what she'd say. She'd probably just laugh at him. "Go talk to your Mr. Garvey," she'd tell him. Or, "Packing your bags for Liberia, Henry? You'd better get far away from here as you can, mouthing off ideas like that!"

But I couldn't help wondering, too, what would happen if we did what Henry wanted us to do.

ELEVEN

Fourth
of July

On the Fourth of July I left my house not long after sunup, to help Aunt Tillie fix Mrs. Bell's show-off cakes for the picnic and barbecue. Mr. Bell's businessmen's club was planning the affair at the county fairgrounds on the north side of town. The meat would be prepared by Mr. Bell's club members — meaning, the work would be done by the Negroes. Other groups were putting out the sweet corn and potato salad and such. Mrs. Bell's Garden Club had promised to provide desserts, and the ladies had all given orders to their cooks to fix something extra special.

Aunt Tillie made two high yellow sponge cakes, each baked in a special pan with a tube in the center, each to be iced with fluffy white frosting. My job was to beat the eggs, which I did until my arm ached and Aunt Tillie took over for me.

When the cakes were finished, Mrs. Bell fitted narrow glass vases in the center holes which were to hold patriotic bouquets of red petunias, white geranium, and blue foxglove, and two little American flags on sticks.

Mr. Bell proposed to drive out to the fairgrounds after lunch on the afternoon of the Fourth, and Aunt Tillie was to follow along with the cakes and all the plates and silverware and so forth, packed in Grandfather Jim's wagon. Grandfather would be available to help with the barbecuing, and Aunt Tillie was to help with the serving. I intended to hurry home and go to the fish fry and pie sale in the church grove — not such a big affair as Juneteenth, but still a good time. Lou Ann and Bessie and other girls my age planned to help our mothers sell pies to raise money for the Household of Ruth, and Poppa's lodge would be making ice cream to benefit their own group. I looked forward to this.

But at the last minute, after we set out a light lunch for the Bells to tide them over until their barbecue supper, Aunt Tillie drew me aside and begged me to go in her place. Her feet hurt, she said; her head ached. She thought she was coming down with something and needed to stay home and rest.

"Henry been talking to you about this?" I asked, kind of suspicious.

"Henry? What's he got to do with my bad headache?" Aunt Tillie snapped. "You go, Rose Lee," she said then, not so snappish. "They'll have fireworks after dark. You might have a good time." I didn't think I would, but I couldn't say no. Besides, she offered me an extra quarter to do it.

Mrs. Bell gave me a shrewd look with her little blue eyes when Aunt Tillie explained the change. "I suppose Rose Lee will do," she said. "She's learning to be a good worker."

Mrs. Bell decided that I shouldn't wear my regular maid's uniform, which was not quite the right thing for a barbecue. Did I have a plain white dress?

"Yessum."

"Wear that, then, Rose Lee. And you won't come dragging in late, will you?"

"No, ma'am." As if I ever had!

It meant I had to run home to change, but Mrs. Bell didn't think about that. Poppa and Momma and Nancy Lee and Lora Lee were ready to leave for the church grove. Mrs. Morgan and Momma and Aunt Susannah had spent all morning baking pies to sell. (If she wasn't any better at baking pies than she was at ironing napkins, they must have had their hands full.) Henry had already left for the fairgrounds, saying he intended to meet Grandfather there. I wasn't sure if I could believe him, after all the fuss he made about not working.

I put on the white dress that once belonged to Catherine Jane and the hurtful white shoes and waited for Grandfather to bring his old mule, Jojo, from the meadow where he was pastured. Grandfather hitched Jojo up to the wagon he used to haul wood and coal and whatever else needed hauling. Grandmother Lila came out to throw an old quilt over the wagon seat so I wouldn't get dirty before I even reached the fairgrounds, and we set off. I tried not to mind too much, and Momma promised to save me some catfish and a slice of peach pie.

First we stopped by Mrs. Bell's house to pick up the baskets of things Mrs. Bell wanted taken out, and the two pretty sponge cakes in cake tins. It was decided that I should ride with one on either side of me on the seat and fix the flower bouquets and the flags in the centers once we reached the pavilion.

Grandfather had to drive the wagon way over on the side of the road, because there were a good many automobiles going the same place we were going. As they passed they stirred up clouds of dust that swirled and settled on us. Among them was Mr. Tom Bell's Packard. He tooted the horn as he swerved around us, and Catherine Jane leaned out the window and waved. Later I saw Edward Bell rush by with some of his friends in the new Model T Ford that was his graduation present, but he took no notice of us. Even if he saw us, he wouldn't wave. Edward talked about Negroes as "niggers" and "coons" right in front of me, as though I was deaf. I paid no mind to him. Or tried.

By the time we reached the fairgrounds, brown dust had sifted down all over my white dress and stuck to my sweaty skin. I wiped it off as best I could and spit on the corner of my hankie to clean my shoes.

The automobiles were parked in a field in ragged rows. Grandfather Jim pulled the wagon in next to them, unhitched Jojo, and let him browse. I took charge of the cake tins, and Grandfather made two trips to the wagon for the other baskets and boxes. Then he went to see about the beef and pork that had been barbecuing since early morning in the pit the colored men had dug and built a fire in the night before.

Mrs. Bell appeared with a red-white-and-blue–striped apron for me to put over my white dress, so that I would look patriotic, and pointed out the dessert table. I was to make sure her two cakes were displayed up front where everybody could see them and then to slice them neatly just before they were to be served.

"Can I trust you to do that, Rose Lee? Not to make a mess of things?"

"Yessum."

I was also to keep watch over the pies and cakes brought by the other ladies of the Garden Club. I knew by sight most of those who came by to drop off their fancy desserts, but of course I gave no sign. That Garden Club luncheon, my first day as a maid, seemed like a long, long time ago.

The young people — Catherine Jane and Edward and their friends — hurried off to the Niagara Plunge, a new bathing pool that was all the rage. I had been serving sliced peaches and a plate of Aunt Tillie's cookies to the Bells on the evening Catherine Jane announced that she needed a new bathing outfit. Her father asked what was wrong with what she already had, but her mother took Catherine Jane's part.

Next she began to go on about how she surely ought to have her hair bobbed if she was going swimming. Her mother was shocked. "Cut your beautiful hair, Catherine Jane? The very idea!"

Catherine Jane was fourteen and willful. I thought she was talking about bobbing her hair just to upset her mother, who held that even wearing her long blond hair combed up and pinned on top of her head was much too grown-up. But compared to a bob, combing it up seemed harmless. Her mother weakened exactly like her father had. "You may comb it up just this once then," Mrs. Bell agreed. "But it's not to be your regular style."

I saw Catherine Jane's pouty expression melt into a sweet smile, and when her parents weren't looking she winked at me.

While the young people swam, the adults settled down to listen to speeches under a tent, open at the sides to admit whatever breeze there was. A whole row of men, some of whom I had served at Mrs. Bell's table, sat on the platform draped with red-white-and-blue bunting, waiting their turn. I fanned a pesky green fly away from the sweet desserts and tried to listen.

Most of the speeches were about Freedomtown and the vote on the bond issue to be taken the next day. Mayor Dixon, the man with the bushy side-whiskers, stepped up to the speakers' stand. I could hear most every word he said and wished I couldn't.

"Citizens of Dillon! The very future of this community depends on your vote, ladies and gentlemen! Let us make Dillon, Texas, a city we can all be proud of!" boomed the mayor.

Then came Dr. Wesley Thompson, the president of the Dillon Academy for Young Ladies, talking about "the future of young womanhood, our most precious treasure."

It was hard to hear this and know that it was my home these men were talking about, that showing pride in Dillon meant getting rid of my family and friends, all of us. Tears ran down my face, and I smeared them away with the back of my hand.

I didn't see Catherine Jane come up alongside me, and I jumped when she spoke my name. Her hair was still damp, dark strands of it stuck to her cheeks. She was wearing some kind of loose robe over her bathing outfit and pretty little sandals on her delicate white feet. Those sandals looked so comfortable. My own feet were aching and burning.

"I came to snitch a piece of pie," she said with a sly grin.

"Probably not allowed to let you have any until afterward," I told her.

"Suppose I just went ahead and took one, Rose Lee. Suppose I just ran away with an entire pie to share with my friends!"

I raised my eyebrows. I knew her momma would not approve of that, but Catherine Jane was obstinate as a mule. "Guess there wouldn't be much I could do to stop you," I said.

"Well, I won't anyway," she said with a sigh. "Those boys are such teases. They sent me over to steal them a pie, and I can bet they wouldn't even share it with me if I did. Or else they'd give me a little bitty piece. They can come and get their own."

She picked up a knife and made as if to carve herself a slice of custard pie. You could see she wasn't used to handling a kitchen knife, bad as Aunt Susannah with the iron. "Guess it would get you in a whole lot of trouble, wouldn't it?"

I just nodded, and she laid the knife down and settled herself on a bench. Having Catherine Jane so close kept me from attending to the speeches, which may have been just as well. I was mightily sick of listening to those men anyway. "Those speeches are boring," she said.

"Sure are," I agreed.

"Rose Lee!" she said suddenly, pointing at the speakers' platform. "Look!"

Miss Emily Firth, who I hadn't seen since

that last time she sketched in the garden, was climbing up the steps, all dressed up in a navy blue skirt, a white shirtwaist, and a red sash. She had on a straw hat, too, with a red-white-and-blue ribbon around it, and she was carrying a little American flag. She walked briskly across the platform and stood next to Mayor Dixon. He looked startled. We could see that people in the audience were startled, too, waiting to see what would happen. Then her voice boomed out through the megaphone she had picked up.

"Ladies and gentlemen!" she said loudly, her clear voice carrying plainly all the way over to the pavilion where Catherine Jane and I pressed forward to hear every word. "My name is Emily Firth, and I want to speak to you about the other side of this issue. I want to talk to you this afternoon about the rights of the Negroes in this community who have served you so faithfully and so well for so many years."

Before she could say much more, people in the audience began to call out "Go home, Yankee!" and other things I couldn't make out. Within a minute or two Mayor Dixon and Dr. Wesley Thompson had stepped forward and made a great show of thanking her for her interest and announcing that everyone would now rise and sing "The Star Spangled Banner." The Dillon High School Band quickly began to play, and everyone stood up while the Mayor held a big American flag and Mr. Tom Bell, who was also on the platform, waved the Lone Star flag of Texas. Two men I didn't know escorted Miss Firth from the stage, one on either side of her, gripping her arms as though they expected her to try to run away. She hung onto her little American flag.

"She told me she was planning to do this," Catherine Jane breathed. "I didn't believe her."

I couldn't think what to say. I had never heard a white person, a white *woman*, speak out for Negroes like that before. I thought she was very brave. First Henry in church, then Aunt Susannah at the Juneteenth picnic, and now Miss Emily Firth — all speaking out. There had never been a time like this in Dillon, I was sure about that.

"I go to see her sometimes, although I'm not supposed to. It was going to be for art lessons, but to tell you the truth, I don't have much talent. So we just sit and talk. She knew she was going to be fired, so she decided she'd go ahead and make this speech anyway, even though she knew it wouldn't do much good. You saw how people reacted."

"I bet she was scared," I said. "I would have been."

"She told me her mother was a suffragist,

one of those women who worked for years to get the right to vote for women. Her mother even got sent to prison, and she used to go on hunger strikes. Once she and some other women chained themselves to the cell door and refused to come out. So Miss Emily comes from a family that's used to speaking up for what they believe. But I never thought I'd see anything like this! My mother and daddy must be fit to be tied!"

"Mine are, too," I reminded her. "For a different reason."

She turned to look at me, her eyes as big and blue as her china doll's. "Are you going to try to stop them from making you move?" she asked.

I dared to look her boldly in the face. "I don't know there's anything *to* do," I said. "Poppa and some of the men wrote letters, but it didn't help any."

"I'd stop them, if I were you," she said. "I wouldn't let anybody take away my home."

"Sometimes there's nothing you can do, Catherine Jane," I said, thinking that Henry would surely agree with her way of thinking and not with mine. "Sometimes you just got to do what people tell you you got to do."

"Maybe so." She sighed. "I better go."

I watched her hurry to rejoin her friends at

the Niagara Plunge, her concern about the fate of Freedomtown seeming to be forgotten.

The speeches droned on through the hot afternoon. I wondered where Miss Firth had gone. The same green fly buzzed, and I slapped him dead. There was not even the slightest breeze. I felt sleepy.

But I woke up in a hurry when Henry showed up at the pavilion. Lester Sledge was with him, and Cora's husband, Raymond, and a couple of other young men I recognized. "Come on, Rose Lee," Henry said.

"Where?"

"Away from here." He jerked his head. "Come on, we don't have all day."

"Can't. I'm helping Mrs. Bell. I thought you were over at the barbecue pit with Grandfather."

"We were, but not now. Told you, Rose Lee, let those white folks do their own work. Just this one day would teach them a lesson."

"Where's Grandfather?" I asked.

"He's staying over there. He's just too old and too stubborn. It's young folks like us got to do something. You coming with us?"

Part of me wanted to, but part of me was too scared. Not just of what the white folks would do, but of what Grandfather and Momma and Poppa would say. So I just stood there, my heart jumping up and down inside my chest.

"Somebody coming," Lester muttered.

"Never mind," Henry said to me. "It's all right, Rose Lee," he added softly, and before I could say anything, Henry and his friends were gone.

AFTER THE speeches ended, everyone drifted lazily toward the pavilion. While they ate their fill of barbecue and the rest, a band entertained with a concert of patriotic music. As darkness fell and it got a bit cooler, the white folks settled back to admire the fireworks that began to bloom and sparkle in the dark sky. But I had no time to watch. I had to help Grandfather and the others clean up. At last we put Mrs. Bell's cake tins and other things in Grandfather's wagon and started the trip back to town.

I didn't mind too much that we didn't stay to watch the fireworks. I enjoyed riding alongside my grandfather behind Jojo's switching tail. Since I stopped helping out in the garden and began serving inside, I didn't have much time to talk to him anymore.

"I ever tell you, Rose Lee, about how I come to marry your grandmaw?" he asked.

I had been half asleep on the seat next to

him, but I heard a story coming on, and I straightened up to listen.

"I had a vision. You know how it says in the Bible, 'Your old men shall dream dreams, your young men shall see visions,' well, I had me this vision. I was just a young man, and I had gone up to Kansas to cut wheat, and one night in a dream, a voice told me to go home and marry either Miss Lila Huckaby or Miss Addie Price, whichever one I saw first. I didn't even wait for morning, that vision was so powerful. I got up, caught the next train down, and since it was a Sunday, I went straight to church meeting. And who should be standing up front in the choir but Miss Lila!"

I loved stories like this. I leaned against his shoulder as Grandfather went on, "Wasn't five minutes after I saw your grandmaw standing up front, pretty as a picture, singing so nice, that Miss Addie Price come in with her daddy and set down directly across from me. Dressed fit to kill, she was, all ribbons and bows and a new flowered hat. And I was mighty tempted, because I knew that daddy of hers owned a lot of good farmland. Mr. Price was rich, by our reckoning, and Mr. Huckaby was just a poor laboring man like me. But I was true to my vision. I saw Miss Lila first, and Miss Lila it would be. I asked her to walk with me that afternoon. Three months later we got married."

"But what ever happened to Miss Addie, Grandfather?" I couldn't resist asking.

"Married some fella from down around Fort Worth, I believe. I forgot all about her, soon as I married your grandmaw."

Jojo kept up his steady plodding. We were on Oak Street, almost at the Bells' house. "Did you have any more visions, Grandfather?"

"No," he said with a sigh. "That's for young men, like Henry. Now I'm an old man, and all I can do is dream."

"But what do you dream about?" I insisted.

"I dream that we won't have to move. That we can stay where we are."

"That's not Henry's vision," I said.

"I know. I know."

The courthouse clock that Catherine Jane could see from her third-floor balcony was striking ten when Jojo pulled up at Mrs. Bell's kitchen door. It seemed we were the first ones back.

Independence Day was almost over. Tomorrow the white people of Dillon would vote on the bond issue, and soon we'd know for sure if we would have to leave Freedomtown. There wasn't much doubt in my mind which way it would go and that Grandfather's dream would be only that.

TWELVE

Henry

MOMMA AND POPPA were sitting out on our veranda, waiting for me to come home.

"Too bad you missed the fish fry," Momma said. "We sold out all our pies, but I did manage to save you one little slice."

"What about the barbecue?" Poppa asked.

"Lots of speeches," I said. I told them about Miss Emily Firth. I didn't tell them about Henry.

"Why don't you go on to bed, Rose Lee," Momma said. "You look all tuckered out."

I said good night and went inside and hollowed a space for myself next to my sisters. For a time it seemed I was too tired to sleep. I heard the bedsprings squeak when my parents climbed into their bed, and then everything was quiet and I fell asleep.

Sometime before sunup I awoke, needing to go to the toilet. There was a chamber pot under the bed for nighttime use, but I preferred to go out to the privy at the back of our lot near the alley. My eyes burning from tiredness and lack of sleep, I stumbled out the back door and across our yard webbed with clotheslines toward the wooden shack. I was not halfway there when I saw a sight that caused me to stop where I was and cry out.

Staggering up the alley behind our house was a terrible figure, a man whose entire body was covered in some strange white stuff. He tottered rather than walked, his legs locked at the knees, his arms held stiffly away from his body. He groaned. I was about to turn and run back into the house when he called out to me.

"Rose Lee!"

I recognized Henry's voice. I waited, frozen, as he approached me stiff legged and stopped in front of me, swaying. His body seemed to be plastered with feathers, like some huge, horrible bird. I crept closer. I could see now that he was plastered all over with black stuff, and chicken feathers were stuck to it. Only his eyes and mouth were free of feathers.

"Rose Lee, help me," he moaned.

"What happened?" I tried not to scream.

"Last night," he muttered. He could hardly speak. "Caught me. Fairgrounds. Tarred and feathered. Hot tar. Burned."

He fainted, dropped to the ground at my feet. Then I did begin to scream, but I didn't shriek more than once before Momma and Poppa came running out in their nightclothes. "Oh!" was all Momma said, and Poppa said, "We have to get him inside."

Momma sent me for a clean sheet, and we gently rolled Henry onto it and bunched it up at the ends. Poppa took one end and Momma and I seized the other, and heavy as he was, we managed to carry him that way, careful not to bump, and laid him out on his cot.

Momma fought back tears when she began to examine him. Gingerly she pulled at a few of the chicken feathers that stuck to the black tar coating every inch of him, head to foot. "Rose Lee," she said calmly. "Run get the coal oil."

I came back with the can of kerosene to find her ripping our bedsheets into rags. Working carefully, she dipped a little coal oil onto the rag and wiped it on a bit of Henry's skin. Little by little she gently scrubbed away the awful black stuff. The hot tar had burned his skin in patches, and sometimes the skin peeled off no matter how careful Momma tried to be. Henry was awake now, gritting his teeth against the pain. When Momma had used up all our old sheets, she sent me to Grandmother Lila's for more. "But don't tell her why you need them. No sense getting her all upset."

But Grandmother looked at me and knew in a wink something was wrong. "Never mind making up a story, Rose Lee," she said. "I'll just come along with you."

"Fetch Dr. Ragsdale," Momma said later, sitting back on her heels as the pile of tarry rags grew beside her.

The sun was up by then, and it was starting to get hot. Little puffs of dust spurted up from my bare heels, and sweat trickled down my arms. When I reached the doctor's house, the fanciest in Freedom but still nothing to compare to Mrs. Bell's, Mrs. Ragsdale was in the backyard watering her garden. She waited for me to come up onto the veranda and catch my breath.

"It's my brother Henry. He's been tarred and feathered, and Momma says he's burned pretty bad."

She held the back door open for me. The doctor, in his shirt sleeves and suspenders, sat at the kitchen table, sipping coffee. I repeated my story. "You run on back home, Rose Lee," he said. "I'll be right along."

After I told Momma, I sat down on the front steps to wait until Dr. Ragsdale appeared, carrying his black leather bag. I showed him where to go and went back to sit on the steps again. People passed by our house on their way to work, nodding and calling out good morning. Some who knew us well stopped to speak to Momma or Poppa. When they did, I told them about Henry.

The word spread quickly. Before Momma had finished treating Henry's burns with Dr. Ragsdale's soothing balm and lightly bandaging them with the clean sheets Grandmother Lila tore into strips with her teeth, most of Freedom had heard about my brother.

It wasn't until later that morning, when I was to leave for Mrs. Bell's, that Henry was finally able to talk about what had happened.

Some young white fellows found out that Henry was urging people to quit and let the white folks do their own work. The boys chased him and Lester and Raymond and caught Henry. He thought the others got away.

I was in my room, straining to hear as he told his story to Poppa and Momma. The boys had put him in their car and driven him somewhere on the outskirts of town. They stripped him of all his clothes and ridiculed him and ordered him to dance for them. When he refused, they tied him to a tree. Some of them left and came back with a bucket of tar. They built a fire to melt it and smeared the hot tar all over him with a brush and doused him with pillow ticks full of feathers. They told him to run if he didn't want to be hog-tied to a rail and carried off and dumped someplace.

He had run, best he could, with the horrible stuff all over him and the pain from the burns. His idea had been to hide out for a while and try to get the mess off himself, but he couldn't. And so he had headed home. It had been a long ways to go in his condition. That's when I found him in our backyard. I squeezed my eyes shut while he talked.

"Why?" I heard Poppa ask. "Why do something so foolish, boy?"

Because he had a vision, I thought to myself. Young men have visions, old men dream dreams.

If Henry said anything, I didn't hear.

Then Henry slept. I tiptoed fearfully past

his cot, where he lay looking like one of those Egyptian mummies I had seen in my schoolbook, and went to work at Mrs. Bell's.

Aunt Tillie had been there since early morning, washing up the dishes Grandfather and I had dropped off the night before.

"Something bad happened," I said as I slipped quietly in through the kitchen door.

I told her what happened to Henry, leaving out the part about Cora's husband, Raymond.

"That Raymond with him?"

"Uh. Yessum." No sense lying; she'd find out.

"Fools! All of them." She shot me an angry look, but I knew it wasn't me she was mad at. She was mad at Raymond and Henry and at the whole situation that made them act this way. "Go set the table."

"IT WILL BE a splendid opportunity for your people, Tillie," Mrs. Eunice Bell was saying to Aunt Tillie. It was the day after the vote was taken, and we knew for sure we had to leave Freedomtown. We were in the kitchen, getting ready to serve dinner, and I moved in a daze, trying to bury my sadness.

"Yessum," Aunt Tillie said.

"It's always pleasant to have a new home," Mrs. Bell went on. "There's been such a problem in your area with flooding after the rains. All that mud! The city will buy you out, at fair prices, I'm sure, and then you'll have a chance to build new houses, much better than those shacks you're living in now."

Shacks? I felt as though she had slapped me. Maybe to her eyes they were shacks, but not to ours. Freedom wasn't anything like Dogtown.

"Yessum," Aunt Tillie said in a flat voice, not looking up from the tomatoes she was slicing onto a plate.

It was not usual, Mrs. Bell being there. Mostly she didn't come around the kitchen much, just enough to speak with Aunt Tillie about what dishes she wanted prepared and to give Aunt Tillie a list of things to get from the store. Aunt Tillie could read a little, but I always helped her go over the list.

Mrs. Bell left. Aunt Tillie kept on slicing, singing softly as she worked. You could tell how Aunt Tillie felt by what she was singing. That day it was "Nobody knows the trouble I see, Nobody knows but Jesus." I stepped over and stood close beside my aunt. She wiped her hands on her apron and put her stout arms around me and pulled my head close to her chest, and we stood that way for I don't know how long.

"We going to be just fine, honey, don't you worry," she said. "Now you get yourself ready and go in there and do a good job serving for the lady, like you always do."

But it was hard, very hard. I served dinner as Mr. and Mrs. Bell and Catherine Jane planned a vacation trip they intended to take on the train, all the way up to Chicago. What was happening to us had nothing to do with them. They didn't care about us losing our place, or about Henry, still bandaged up and in pain. Holding out a plate of pork chops for Edward, I wondered if he was one of the young fellows who caught my brother and did what they did to him. Edward took the thickest chop and drowned it in gravy.

I decided I didn't *want* to know.

THAT NIGHT when I got home I learned that the men of Freedom were having a special meeting. There were too many to get together in Poppa's barbershop, and they had gathered at the Masonic Hall above the Sun-Up Café. No women were supposed to be there, and I had to wait for Poppa to come home and tell us about it.

"There's nothing we can do, Elvie," he said, sitting at the kitchen table under the coal-oil lamp and holding a big cup of coffee in his two hands. "We wrote them that letter, asking them to pay fair prices for our homes, but Pastor Mobley says they'll pay as little as they think they can get away with, and we won't get near enough to build anything nice as we've got right now."

"But *where*, Charles?" my mother asked, her voice thick from tears. "Where will we build? Surely not in Dogtown."

Dogtown was the awfulest place in Dillon, nothing but leaky, tumbledown tin shacks. It made me sick to think we might have to go live there.

"Don't know where yet. But it will work out. It won't be Dogtown, I promise you that." He moved his coffee cup around in circles on the oilcloth. "Dr. Ragsdale's going away," he said at last. "Told us tonight he's moving his family to Cairo, Illinois, where his wife is from."

"But he can't!" Momma said. "Now we'll have no colored doctor, and we'll have to look for a white doctor who'll treat us."

"I know that," Poppa said. "If anything ever

happens again like happened to Henry, no white doctor would come to our house to take care of him."

"*Now* you gonna listen to me?"

Our heads jerked up. It was Henry, wrapped up like a mummy in his sheet bandages, looming in the doorway. He was a scary sight. Momma let out a little cry, and Poppa jumped up. "Better lie down, son," he said.

"When you gonna pay attention?" Henry demanded, refusing to budge. "We got to leave here. We got to go to Africa."

And much as it pained me, I was thinking Henry was right — we did have to leave. But I surely did not want to go to Africa.

THIRTEEN

House Cleaning

Two TAXICABS arrived to carry Mr. and Mrs. Bell and Edward and Catherine Jane and all their baggage to the railroad depot. I watched from the kitchen window while Grandfather helped the drivers to load their suitcases. They planned to be gone for two weeks. Suddenly Catherine Jane appeared in the kitchen, dressed in her new traveling outfit.

"Rose Lee," she whispered. "Come here. I have to talk to you, quickly, before Mother sees." She motioned me to follow her back into the pantry while Tillie gave me a sour look. Catherine Jane handed me an envelope addressed to Miss Emily Firth. "I want you to deliver this for me today," she said. "Please."

"Yes, Catherine Jane."

"I'd have taken it myself, but Mother and Daddy have absolutely forbidden me to have anything further to do with her. They'd be furious if they knew I had written her this note. It's just to thank her and wish her well, so she doesn't go away thinking everybody in Dillon despises her for speaking out."

"I'll take it," I promised.

"I'm sure she expected to be fired from her job for telling people to vote against the park, but still! It makes me sad that I'll never see her again, and I didn't even have a chance to say good-bye. I'm sure she'll be gone by the time we get back."

I slipped the envelope into my apron pocket as Tillie hollered from the kitchen, "Catherine Jane! Your folks out there looking for you!"

"Coming!"

Catherine Jane climbed into the back of the taxicab with her momma, and Grandfather sat up front next to the driver, George Ellis, to make sure everything got put on the train to Chicago. My uncle Walter drove the second cab with Edward and Mr. Bell.

Soon as they were gone, we started ripping that house apart.

Grandfather and Aunt Tillie and my two aunts, Flora and Vinnie, had been instructed to clean the Bells' house from top to bottom while they were away. Each Thursday all year 'round Aunt Flora dusted and mopped every room in the house, but this was different, and Aunt Vinnie came to help out. Windows were to be washed inside and out, carpets taken up and beaten, floors stripped of old wax and shined with new, woodwork wiped clean with soap and water, curtains washed, ironed, and hung up again, bedding aired. Even Aunt Flora and Aunt Vinnie couldn't do it all themselves, and Aunt Tillie fussed that Grandfather Jim was too old for such work. Aunt Tillie told me this happened every summer when the Bell family went away on their vacation. She called me in to help as well. I didn't mind much. I would get paid an extra quarter for my work, and I was glad about that.

Aunt Flora's plan was to start on the top floor and work our way down. She sent me into Mr. Bell's smoker to dust his library. I was to take out each book, wipe off the fine leather binding and the gilded edges, and make sure the book got put back on the shelf in the proper order.

Aunt Flora opened the windows to get rid of the smell of stale tobacco. Aunt Vinnie took down the dark red draperies and threw them right out the window to Aunt Tillie in the backyard who hung them up to air. Grandfather rolled up the Oriental carpet and carried it out. Light and fresh air streamed into the smoker. I worked my way along the top shelf, standing on the ladder Grandfather set up for me, sometimes pausing to leaf through one of the books, though few interested me. When I reached the end of one shelf, I moved to the one below it.

When I had finished the books, I dusted the framed pictures hanging on the walls, hunting scenes with birds and deer and dogs and horses. At one end of the bookshelves was a glass case full of guns, locked up tight and no key in view. We were not to clean that, I supposed. At the opposite end was a narrow cupboard, similar to the gun case but with a plain wooden door. Idly I turned the brass knob—it would have to be polished, I could see that—and pulled it open.

The cupboard was almost empty, except for one thing: a long white robe hung on a hook. I took the robe down and looked at it, hoping it was not what I knew it to be. Then I noticed something else draped on a second hook all the way in the back: a white hood, pointed at the top, two holes cut for eyes. My hands shaking, I spread out the pointed hood and the robe with its round embroidered patch over the left breast on the leather sofa and stared at them. Soot streaked the sleeves, as though whoever wore that robe had been near a fire.

The robe and hood belonged to Mr. Tom Bell, I was sure. That meant Mr. Bell was a member of the Ku Klux Klan. That meant he was one of the dozens of men we had watched marching silently through Freedom to burn the cross in our church grove. He could have been the one who lit the fire. I shuddered.

With shaking hands, I put the robe and hood back in the cupboard exactly as I found them and shut the door. I bolted from the room and ran down the stairs to the second floor, smack into my aunt Flora, who was carrying an armload of lace curtains out of Mr. and Mrs. Bell's bedroom. "What's wrong, Rose Lee? You look like you've seen a ghost!"

"Nothing," I lied. "I just don't want to be in that room anymore."

Aunt Flora eyed me, her face making a question that she didn't ask. I turned my head. I didn't want to tell her what I had seen.

"I finished all the books up there. Let me clean Catherine Jane's room," I pleaded. "I'll be extra careful."

"Don't you be going through her things now," Aunt Flora warned. "Just clean what you see."

Maybe another time I would have been happy to be back in the room where I had such pleasant times as a young child. But things had changed and I didn't feel so curious anymore. The dolls had all been put away somewhere. Now Catherine Jane collected china dogs of all kinds, they filled the shelves where the dolls had been, and I carefully dusted each one. Some of the books I remembered were still there: *Alice's Adventures in Wonderland* and *Through the Looking Glass*. But *A Child's Garden of Verses* was gone.

Next to the books I found two albums in which she had pasted invitations and souvenirs and newspaper clippings describing events she had attended. There was an article about Helen Keller, the blind lady, who came with Annie Sullivan and gave a lecture at Dillon Academy, and a program for the evening. Across the top of the program she had scribbled, "Fascinating. CJB." Sometimes she pasted a small white card on the black album page next to the clipping and added details. "Breathtaking" and "Electrifying" were words she favored.

On another page she had stuck ticket stubs from the Rialto and the Embassy, the motion-picture theater where she and her brother often went with their friends.

I knew Aunt Flora would be upset if she

found me looking through Catherine Jane's albums, so I busied myself taking the ruffled curtains down from her windows and bundling up the pink counterpane and pillow shams to take home to Momma to wash. I rolled up the oval hooked rug and dragged it out into the hall. I laid the ivory-backed hairbrush and mirror and matching buttonhook and comb on the bed and added the embroidered bureau scarf to the pile of wash. Little by little her pretty bedroom became plain and ordinary, like mine.

Soon as we were finished for the day, I went home and put on a clean dress and went looking for Miss Emily Firth. By the address Catherine Jane had written on the envelope, I knew she boarded with Mrs. Walker in the big white house with pillars across from the Academy at the north end of Edwards Street. Mrs. Walker peered through the screen door at me. "I have a letter for Miss Firth," I explained.

"All right," she said. "I'll give it to her." I could tell by the look on Mrs. Walker's face that she didn't have a high opinion of her boarder.

"I have to give it to her myself."

"Wait here."

In a minute Miss Firth came and unhooked the screen door. "Rose Lee! I'm so glad to see you. I have something I've been wanting to give you. Come on upstairs to my room."

"She can wait for you on the back porch," Mrs. Walker, who'd been watching, said in a mean voice.

"I'm sorry, Rose Lee," said Miss Firth. "I'll be right back."

I sat on the steps by the kitchen and waited, thinking that Mrs. Walker could use some help in her garden, but it sure wasn't going to be me. When Miss Firth came out, I noticed she carried a flat bundle tied with string. She sat down beside me.

"Catherine Jane Bell sent you a letter," I said, handing her the envelope. "She says you're leaving soon."

"Indeed I am. Tomorrow morning. I've just about finished packing." She laid the bundle in my lap. "This is a sketchbook, Rose Lee, and my box of drawing pencils—they're not new, but there's still plenty of use left in them. I'm so sorry we never got to have those art classes, because I really do believe you have talent. Now," she said, talking so fast I didn't have a chance to say anything, "I've had an idea and I want you to make me a promise, Rose Lee. I think you should make a record of Freedom-town. Will you do that?"

"A record?" I had no idea what she meant.

"I want you to make a drawing of every

home in Freedomtown, every church, every school, every little corner that means something to you. Something for everyone to remember by. When the city's park plan goes through, there will be nothing left of Freedomtown in a few months. They'll move or knock down everything there that is precious to you."

Her voice rose with excitement. I figured Mrs. Walker was standing in the kitchen with her ear glued to the door, listening to every word. Well, let her, I thought. "So you must work quickly, Rose Lee. On every page, a drawing of a building, and in the corners of the pages the little extra things, like a nice window or a bit of decoration on the porch. And don't forget the gardens! I imagine that your grandfather's is very special. Someday that sketchbook may be all there is to show that Freedomtown ever existed. Will you do that?"

"Yes, ma'am," I said. "I surely do thank you for the sketchbook and pencils. I promise that I'll put all of Freedomtown in it as best I can, and it won't be forgotten."

Then because I was afraid I'd start to cry if I stayed with her any longer, afraid she might, too, I jumped down off the steps and ran all the way home, hugging the bundle to my chest.

FOURTEEN

More Trouble

THE JULY DAYS wore on, long and hot. There was no rain. Dust seeped into everything.

In spite of the heat and the drought Grand-father Jim managed to keep his Garden of Eden blooming with buckets of Momma's rinse water, which Aunt Susannah and I carried to him.

My aunt was spending more time at our house, and she even offered to help Momma with the cooking. But she either burned it or didn't cook it enough or mixed the wrong things together, reciting poetry the whole time. She thought it was time I learned some poetry by heart and got me started on a poem by an English lady, Mrs. Browning.

"How do I love thee? Let me count the ways," she'd have me saying out loud as we walked down Logan Street, struggling to keep the buckets from slopping over. "I love thee to the depth and breadth and height, My soul can reach," and so on.

"Glorious, just glorious!" she'd say. "Can you hear the music of that, Rose Lee?"

"Yessum. But it hits me as awful sad. 'I shall but love thee better after death.' Seems like she ought to love him while he's still alive."

"Sad, but beautiful, Rose Lee."

I wondered if she still thought about John, the white man she hadn't married. But I didn't ask her. Every Sunday she got dressed up in her red dress and red shoes and carried her red parasol, and I figured it was to keep herself cheered up. The poetry she liked to recite surely wasn't going to do it.

Then one Sunday morning as we were walking home from church she announced, "Time for me to think about going back up to St. Louis. I ought to start preparing for school."

"Do you have to?" I asked. "Why don't you stay here?"

"Because that's my home, Rose Lee. Much

as I've come to love being here with all of you."

"We'll be sorry to see you go, Sister," Momma said, and I believe she really meant it, even though she never could quite get used to Aunt Susannah's city ways. "You can tell she's never had to do for a family," Momma said to me more than once when Aunt Susannah burned the biscuits or, worse, scorched some white lady's bedsheets when she tried to help Momma with the ironing.

At the end of July, Catherine Jane came back from her vacation trip to Chicago, bringing with her a whole bagful of stylish new dresses, cut so narrow and straight they made her look like a boy, except for a flurry of pleats around the bottom and a belt draped all the way down around her hips. When her mother wasn't home she invited me up to her bedroom to look at them, spread out on her bed.

"Aren't they exquisite, Rose Lee?" she said, picking them up one by one to hold against her body.

Exquisite must be a word they use in Chicago, I thought. Soon she would be passing on to me her old clothes that weren't in style, or grown-up enough. Weren't *exquisite*.

"If only Mother would let me bob my hair!" she went on, lifting a lock of her long blond hair. "All the girls in Chicago do."

"Your hair's mighty pretty like it is." I thought of how every single one of the ladies in Freedom spent hours with oil and a hot comb, trying to straighten their hair and make it lie smooth like Catherine Jane's.

Now that they were back, I was serving in Mrs. Bell's dining room again. But when I had a spare moment I worked on my promise to Miss Firth. When I had opened the sketchbook she gave me, I found the drawing she made of Grandfather and me in Mrs. Bell's garden and determined to do everything I could to honor my promise. If anything of Freedom was to be preserved, I was the one who had to do it. With Mr. and Mrs. Watson and Dr. Ragsdale's family determined to leave and others thinking about it, I knew I had to begin in earnest.

At first I had no plan: I just went out and drew whatever caught my eye, taking care to label it with the address and the names of the people who lived there. I began with the homes of people I didn't know well because I didn't feel as bad about those places as I did about my own home and Grandfather Jim's and Forgiveness Baptist Church and the Booker T. Washington School, where my momma insisted I had to start going again in a few weeks. I always liked school and was glad that she didn't think my earning money for the family was more important.

Meantime, the talk in Poppa's barbershop became more intense. One by one the people of Freedom had been told to come to City Hall to find out how much money the council intended to pay them for their homes. And one by one they stopped by the barbershop to complain bitterly about the council's shabby offers. When it was Mr. Lipscomb's turn, he asked for nine thousand dollars for his ten-room boardinghouse, but the councilmen needed only a few minutes to decide that it was worth a little better than half that amount, take it or leave it.

"What can I do with that?" he asked the men gathered somberly in the barbershop, his eyes watering. Angrily he wiped away the tears. "No way I can rebuild a boardinghouse for that amount of money."

Mr. Tolivar, who owned the grocery and dry-goods store, didn't fare much better. "That's that," he said angrily. "I intend to leave. We'll go back to my wife's home in Kansas. I believe we'll receive better treatment there. This town is a low-down disgrace."

The men shook their heads. Mr. Lipscomb's boardinghouse and Mr. Tolivar's store were among the most valuable properties in Freedom. If those men were going to get only half what their places were worth, everyone knew the rest would fare no better, and maybe worse. Poppa and some of the other men discussed going to Dallas to hire a lawyer who would appeal the case for them and "show those white men we are not to be trifled with." But in the end they didn't do it. Dallas lawyers were known to be high priced.

Almost every night Henry tried to persuade the men in the barbershop to join the Universal Negro Improvement Association. Slowly my brother recovered, but his left leg wouldn't straighten out right where the scars were, so Mr. Alexander wouldn't take him back at the brickyard. Grandfather offered to teach him how to take care of Mrs. Bell's garden. "I'll be thinking about retirement one of these days," Grandfather said. "If you learn good, the job is yours." Henry didn't want to do it. He carried on about how he wasn't going to be any white woman's field nigger, but in the end he agreed. He had to, to bring home some money.

"We must stand together against the will of the white man," he lectured the men in the barbershop. "If every one of us stands firm, we will prevail."

My father and his customers listened to Henry, wagging their heads slowly from side to side. "And when you defy them, are you prepared to suffer more of what you have already suffered?" Pastor Mobley asked him. "Perhaps to watch others in your family and your community suffer what you have suffered — or worse?"

Henry gazed past the preacher, as though he hadn't even heard him. "Then," Henry said in his soft growl, "we must make plans to return to Africa. To a land of our own." But nobody else sided with Henry, at least not out loud.

Early in August, the City Council of Dillon invited a delegation of businessmen, including Mr. Webster, owner of the Sun-Up Café, to inspect the area called The Flats. The council thought this would be a fine place to relocate their community, just as Mr. Alexander said.

"I tell you, it's a mighty bad location," Mr. Webster reported to the men in the barbershop. "Too far from town, too close to the cesspool. It floods every spring. How can I have a restaurant in such a place?"

The men shook their heads. Nobody even mentioned Dogtown as a possibility.

Then Poppa and Mr. Lipscomb and some others began to travel on their own around the countryside in Uncle Walter's taxicab, searching for a place for us to settle and rebuild. They came back talking about an unsettled area on the north side of town not far from the fairgrounds called Buttermilk Hill. There were trees there, Poppa told us, and although it was not as close to the center of Dillon as Freedom was and people would have to travel farther to their work, it was not bad. And the white farmer was hard up for cash and willing to sell. Mr. Lipscomb sounded hopeful.

The next thing we heard was that Mr. Lipscomb had gone ahead and put money down on a big piece of land in Buttermilk Hill and that he planned to move his boardinghouse there along with half a dozen little houses he owned and rented out to some of the poorer families in Freedom.

"Maybe we could find a piece of property up there, too," Poppa said, and for the first time Momma looked a little cheered. Even Grandfather talked about moving to Buttermilk Hill, although Grandmother Lila still stubbornly insisted she was not going *anywhere*.

"If white folks want me to move, they can go ahead and move me. I won't interfere. Won't help 'em none, either." Grandfather Jim just smiled at that. He didn't bother to argue with her. Grandmother Lila was about the only one in Freedom who was never of two minds about what to do.

As soon as we would find out what we would be paid for our property, Poppa decided, we would begin to make preparations. Poppa and Grandfather worked on figuring a way to move our present houses up to Buttermilk Hill, if the city would furnish the mules, so as not to go to the expense of building new ones. I liked that idea.

Everybody seemed hopeful again except for my brother. Henry just laughed when the subject came up, a short, bitter laugh. "Might as well forget that," Henry said when I asked him. "White folks not going to let us move to Buttermilk Hill. The Flats is the only place they'll let us live. There and Dogtown."

As it turned out, Henry was right.

Mr. Lipscomb came by our house late one night after the barbershop was closed. He sat at the kitchen table, shaking with fear or anger or maybe both. Momma fixed him a cup of coffee and cut him a piece of pie. I slipped from my room to listen.

Three men had come to visit his boarding-house, he said, white men, claiming to represent the city of Dillon. "You are not welcome in Buttermilk Hill," they told him, "and if you don't want trouble, go where you been told to go. And that applies to others like you," they added. "We don't want Negroes in that part of town."

"What did you tell them?" Poppa asked.

"I said I already paid for the land, and I intend to move to Buttermilk Hill." He stared at his big square hands, folded on our kitchen table. Momma traveled back and forth with the percolator, to give herself something to do.

"We're going, too," Poppa said in a quiet voice.

"No!" Momma cried. "Charles, no, it's not worth it. I don't want more trouble."

But I saw the muscle working in Poppa's jaw, and I knew her pleading wouldn't change anything. My stomach tightened.

The very next day Mr. Lipscomb brought a paper he had found nailed to his front door when he went home. Mr. Webster, who had also made up his mind to move his café to Buttermilk Hill, got one, too: "Negroes Take Notice," the crudely printed note began, "No moving to Buttermilk Hill or anywheres near. If you already bought property there, sell it. Understand?"

More notices were found nailed to the doors of Forgiveness Baptist, Mt. Olive AME, and Booker T., as we called our school.

Mr. Lipscomb was the richest man in Freedom next to Mr. Morgan, the undertaker, and the one with the most influence, next to Pastor Mobley. "What are you going to do?" everyone asked him. If Mr. Lipscomb knew the answer, then others, like Poppa and Grandfather Jim, would know, too.

"Look for another place," he said, shrugging his massive shoulders. "Buttermilk Hill isn't the only decent place in Dillon. I've been looking at a piece of property on Highland Avenue that might do."

I knew I'd have to hurry up my drawing. Soon people would begin to leave.

The next night my father and mother and many of our neighbors gathered at City Hall to ask about the amount of money they had been told they would receive. As they stood waiting a group of white men filed silently through the door of the meeting room. One of the men, who I recognized as Mr. Tubbs, a neighbor of Mr. Tom Bell's, presented a letter of some kind to the mayor. Mayor Dixon looked it over and coughed. "It's a petition," he said, and then he read it out to all of us who were waiting to learn our fate.

" 'The undersigned property owners and citizens of Court Street and Highland Avenue hereby protest against any attempt to locate the colored population of Freedomtown in our midst.' It's followed by thirty-nine signatures."

A dead calm settled over the high-ceilinged room. An overhead fan stirred the air. Nobody whispered or shuffled feet or made any movement at all. We all sat quiet as statues. It seemed there was no place we could go, except The Flats or Dogtown.

"Well, then," said Mayor Dixon, "if y'all have nothing to say, we'll get on with the business at hand."

It was while most everybody in Freedom was packed into the room at City Hall, or waiting in the hall, or standing outside on the granite steps, that my school caught fire.

MR. PRINCE, the principal, burst in shouting, "The school's on fire!" We all rushed through the double doors and poured out onto the street. Through the trees we could see the orange glow and hurried toward it.

A few people ran home and fetched buckets to carry water from Hickory Creek to throw on the fire, but at that time of summer the creek was nearly dry, and whatever they did manage to scoop up was as useless as spit. Orange and yellow flames danced eerily in the windows of every room in the schoolhouse. Flames burst through the shingled roof, and a fountain of sparks shot toward the sky.

We heard the siren sounding far away in the other part of Dillon, and after what seemed like a long time a firetruck and a pumper arrived. The volunteer firemen in their black rubber coats said a few words to the sweaty men who were still heaving buckets of water at the flames, and they all stood back, shaking their heads.

The schoolhouse was past saving, but the firemen connected their hoses and began to spray the roofs of the houses nearest the school to keep the fire from spreading. They played a stream of water on the flames until they died.

We huddled together and watched. Even after the firemen had packed up their hoses and gone away, we stayed to stare at the glowing ruins. Pastor Mobley and Reverend Delbert from Mt. Olive led us in prayer, and my aunt Tillie began singing, "Oh Mary, don't you weep, don't you mourn," and pretty soon others joined in because, as Aunt Tillie always told me, "It's better to sing than to cry, and singing's as good as praying." So we sang and sang.

I had three reasons to cry: Number one, I understood now how much the white people wanted us gone — we all understood that the fire was no accident. Number two, my school was destroyed. And number three, I had not made a drawing of the schoolhouse in my sketchbook, and now it was no more.

FIFTEEN

Birthday

THE ASHES of my school had turned cold by August sixth, the day Catherine Jane turned fifteen. Her momma and poppa put on a big birthday party for her, and I had little time to grieve for Booker T. A tent was set up on the grass next to the Bells' house for the young people, while the parents were to be entertained in the parlor and dining room.

It was to be a dessert party, Mrs. Bell decided, although Catherine Jane wanted a full dinner served and pouted when her momma said no. I believe Mrs. Bell had in mind something simple, like ice cream and cake and maybe some little candies, but Catherine Jane had other ideas. Instead of a regular birthday cake, marble or sponge or angel food, which Aunt Tillie would have been glad to make, she insisted on having Baked Alaska. I guess she learned about that up in Chicago.

"You start with a layer of pound cake," she explained to Aunt Tillie, "and then you lay a brick of ice cream on top of that and cover the whole thing with meringue and bake it just long enough so the meringue starts to brown."

"You want me to put ice cream in the *oven*, Miss Catherine Jane?" Aunt Tillie demanded. "Can't be done, I'm telling you."

"Yes, it *can*," insisted Catherine Jane. "I know it can, because I had some in Chicago at the Palmer House, and it's absolutely perfect. You just have to do it *fast*, Tillie."

"I don't know about those Palmers in Chicago, whoever they are, but I say it can't be done, and that's that."

"Mother*rrrr!*"

So we baked pound cake for the bottom of the Baked Alaska, and then we churned the ice cream and packed it in a mold and set it in the freezer part of the electric icebox to harden. We'd have to wait until the next-to-last minute to beat the egg whites and the very *last* minute to put the thing together and set it in the oven long enough to turn gold. Then it was to be put on a silver tray and decorated with fifteen candles and carried out to the guests by me. I hoped it wouldn't melt into some bad mess.

And this was besides the ambrosia — sliced oranges and grated coconut — that Mrs. Bell wanted served in a big crystal bowl, and the regular sponge cake with pink icing that Catherine Jane decided she wanted after all.

The day before we squeezed I don't know how many lemons to make lemonade and colored it pink, too. And made pralines and nougat candies, and little mints tinted pink. All this time Mrs. Eunice Bell bustled in and out of the kitchen, fussing and fussing. Aunt Tillie and I worked ourselves half to death, getting ready for that party.

On Saturday afternoon, Edward and his friends moved the Victrola out on the veranda, and Catherine Jane spent an hour or more deciding exactly which records she wanted to play during the refreshments, and which ones were for dancing afterward. This was something she had learned about in Chicago, too. I wanted to ask her more about Chicago, but there was never a chance. Besides, the questions I had in mind — "Where do the Negroes live? Do they have houses like ours?"—weren't anything I could ask anyway, or that I could expect she'd have the answers to.

Right before the guests were to arrive, while we hurried to put the finishing touches on everything, the house phone suddenly rang in the kitchen. This was something new Mr. Tom Bell had put in, and it startled me so I almost jumped out of my skin. Aunt Tillie picked up a little earpiece and listened. I could hear Catherine Jane say in a tinny voice, "Please send Rose Lee upstairs to help me dress."

Aunt Tillie and I looked at each other. "Like she going to be crowned queen or something," Aunt Tillie muttered.

"I can't go now!" I protested. "We got to do that Baked Alaska!"

"Baked Alaska is for later in the evening," Aunt Tillie said. "It's the main event, Mrs. Bell says. You go."

So I hurried upstairs to see what on earth Catherine Jane wanted.

Catherine Jane, wearing some sort of thin white dressing gown, sat at the ruffled dressing table in her bedroom, her back to me in the doorway, staring at herself in the looking glass. I couldn't believe my eyes.

In one hand she held a pair of scissors, and in the other a hank of her long blond hair. The rest of her hair lay in a tangled heap on the floor. What was left was a chopped-off mess that showed most of her neck.

"Catherine Jane," I gasped. "What — ?"

"I cut it," she said, her voice trembling. "I wanted a bob, and I got one. I'm fifteen years old, and it's my hair and no one can tell me what to do with it, no matter what Mother says, and . . ."

She stopped her little speech and turned toward me, her eyes large and shimmery with grief. "Oh, Rose Lee, what am I going to do?" she wailed.

"I don't know, Catherine Jane," I whispered, imagining what her momma was going to say when she got a look at this.

"Can you help me fix it?" she said, sounding like a little girl with a button off her dress.

"*Fix it?* You want *me* to fix it?"

"Yes," she said. "You know how, don't you? Your father's a barber, isn't he?"

"Yessum, he's a barber, but he doesn't cut ladies' hair, and even if *he* knows how doesn't mean *I* know how."

"Oh, please try! Everyone knows it's impossible to cut your own hair. Here, look at the picture in this magazine, it's exactly the way I want mine. Maybe you can copy it." She showed me the magazine picture. "See — short at the sides, tapered at the back, the bangs swept over like this." As though it was the simplest thing in the world.

I studied the picture and looked at what was left of her hair. There was a big difference between the uneven mess in front of me and the sleek hairdo in the magazine. She handed me the scissors. "Mother's sewing scissors," she said. "It was all I could find."

This much I knew: Poppa would never use scissors like this to cut hair. I ran my finger across the blade. "They're dull," I said.

"Oh, Rose Lee," she fretted, "I don't have any others. Just go ahead and cut anyway. Please?" She checked the tiny gold watch on her wrist, a birthday gift from her parents. "Everybody will be here soon, and I haven't even begun to get dressed."

"Give me your comb," I said, "and hold still."

Snip snip snip.

A little tap came at the door. "You about ready, sweetheart?" It was Mrs. Bell. I held my breath. Catherine Jane leaped up from the dressing table and flew to the door, locking it.

"Not quite," she sang out. "Soon, Mother."

She sat down again at her dressing table. "How much longer?" she whispered.

"A little while."

Snip snip snip.

The knock at the door again. "Darling, your guests are beginning to arrive." Mrs. Bell jiggled the doorknob. "What's going on in there, Catherine Jane? I insist that you unlock this door immediately."

"Mother, *please!* I told you I'll be right down." Her footsteps faded down the hall.

Snip snip snip.

I stepped back and studied my work. "All right. That's all I can do." It was short. It was as even as I could make it. It was ugly. Nevertheless, Catherine Jane was thrilled.

"A bob!" she squealed. "A real, grown-up bob!" She spun around on her little stool, studying it from all sides in her ivory hand mirror. "Oh, let's hurry, Rose Lee," she said, stepping over the pile of hair clippings. "Would you help me get into this dress?"

It was one she bought in Chicago, but this was the first I had seen her in it—straight as a yardstick with no waist and much too short. Hundreds of tiny glass beads were stitched around the neck to form a glittery flower pattern. She rolled a pair of sheer silk stockings up over her knees and fastened them with elastic garters, and stepped into a pair of pink shoes dyed the same color as the dress. She dabbed a bit of rouge on her lips and sprayed perfume behind each ear.

"Here I go," she said, touching the hair above her bare neck. "Oh, Mother is going to have such a fit!" Head held high, she walked straight out the door and down the curving staircase, to the hall where her parents were greeting the guests. I stopped by the balcony rail to listen.

Her mother screamed. "Oh, my God, my God—just look at her!" she wailed. "What on earth have you done to yourself, Catherine Jane?"

"Bobbed my hair," she replied calm as you please. "I'm grown-up now."

SOMEHOW we got that Baked Alaska put together and into the oven and out again. I poked fifteen candles into the top and lit them with matches and carried it flaming out to the tent where Catherine Jane's friends and their parents and her momma and poppa and brother and *his* friends were gathered around to sing "Happy Birthday."

Everyone gasped when they saw what it was. Catherine Jane blew out the candles, and then quick as anything, Aunt Tillie and I cut it up and put it on little plates and took them around to the guests before it could melt.

I thought to myself, looking at Catherine Jane as I rushed around, that she would someday be a lady to be reckoned with, her in her fashionable Chicago dress and the first young girl in Dillon to bob her hair. After her momma got used to the idea that the long, beautiful hair was gone, she was proud and puffed up that her daughter was first at something, not just the new short skirt but the new short hair as well.

That very night Catherine Jane began to pester her poppa to teach her to drive his automobile. And it was plain she'd get her way, too, just as she did with everything else. Seeing the look on the faces of those older boys as Catherine Jane flitted from one to the next, I knew that if her poppa didn't hurry up and put her behind the wheel himself, she'd coax one of those boys to teach her. Then next year when they enrolled her at the Dillon Academy for Young Ladies she'd be wanting a car of her own. And would probably get it, too.

THAT VERY NIGHT, too, came the news that nearly broke my heart. Bessie Morgan's family made up their minds to leave. It was her momma told the news to the Household of Ruth, and my momma told me when I got home from Catherine Jane's birthday party.

I ran right over to Bessie's, remembering what she had said at Juneteenth — that her poppa wanted to move away but her momma didn't. Bessie's face was all swollen up from weeping. So was her momma's. But her poppa's face looked like one of the dead people he fixed up for a funeral, stiff and waxy. Her momma's sister was married to Mr. Ross, who had a good job at the Academy and was determined to stay in Dillon, and so the whole family, uncles and aunts and cousins, was grieving, those going and those staying behind. It seemed we were all being torn apart by this.

"Where you going, Bessie?" I asked.

"Someplace up north," she said. "I don't even know. Oh, Rose Lee, I don't want to go, but I don't want to stay in Dillon unless it's here in Freedom!"

I put my arms around her. "I know exactly how you feel," I said. To myself I thought, at least all my people are staying. We'll be together.

But as soon as I thought those words I got the awfulest feeling that they might not be true.

I spent every bit of free time I had with Bessie until the day she left. They planned to

182

take some of their things and gave the rest away to relatives and friends. The Household of Ruth helped them get ready. The night before they left the Knights of Pythias held a special dinner for Mr. Morgan, who had been the president of that lodge for five years, and presented him with a pair of gold cuff links. Mr. Morgan packed up his mortician's equipment, and Lester Sledge and Cora's husband, Raymond, offered to drive his extra-fine black hearse to their new home in Topeka, Kansas, while the family came by train.

Mrs. Morgan took the set of china she was partial to, but she gave her bedroom set to her sister, Mrs. Ross. She said she'd just as soon start over new and not carry a lot of old memories with her. Bessie gave Lou Ann and me each a little embroidered pillow, and I gave her a drawing of her house to take along. We hugged each other and promised never to forget one another.

Most everybody who didn't have to be at work someplace turned up to see them off. I was supposed to be at Mrs. Bell's, but Aunt Tillie said I could run over for a few minutes if I wanted to, provided I hurried right back. Uncle Walter drove them to the railroad depot in his taxicab, and a big group followed along to say good-bye.

The train chuffed in and Mr. and Mrs. Morgan and their children climbed onto the car with the COLORED sign on it. Momma and some of the other ladies in the Household of Ruth had packed them a basket of food to eat on the train, and they handed it up to them through the open window when they got to their seats.

"Write to me, Rose Lee!" Bessie called. "You, too, Lou Ann!"

"We will!" I hollered back.

The train lingered only a minute or two and then they were on their way. Lou Ann and I watched it go, holding tight to each other's hands.

SIXTEEN

Sketches

FROM THE DAY our schoolhouse burned, I had begun to draw in earnest. After Bessie and her family left, I did not allow myself rest. I drew and drew. At first I was very slow, laboring over each line and angle, struggling to make the parts fit together right. As time passed, I improved. The test was if people knew right off what I had drawn.

Every morning I rose before daylight to help Momma, and then I left the house with my sketchbook, picked a place, and began to draw. Folks sometimes stopped by to watch. That made me nervous until I got used to it and began to feel easy. I explained how it was Miss Firth's idea to make a book of drawings about Freedomtown. Most heard how she spoke out at the Fourth of July barbecue, and they also heard that she was fired from her job at the Academy for taking our part.

Sometimes the older people of Freedom wanted to talk about their homes, and I got in the habit of making a few notes down in the corner of each drawing, who built the house and when and so on, whatever they thought I should know. They brought me glasses of cool water to drink while I worked, and sometimes they came out with little cakes or a jar of pickle that I was to take to Momma. A few even offered to pay me if I would make a picture of their home for them to keep as a souvenir, and I promised I would, once I had all the houses recorded in my book.

I was pleased when Mrs. Ragsdale asked me to make pictures of the inside of her pretty little house as well as the outside. And she gave me a special tour of the rooms I hadn't seen before. She was especially proud of her parlor with a silk-fringed lampshade and a velvet-covered settee, almost as nice as anything Mrs. Bell had. "Wedding gifts from my family in Cairo," she explained.

Every so often I showed Grandfather my book, slowly filling with drawings.

"Miss Hamer's house," he'd say, studying a sketch. "A good likeness." He turned the page. "And there's Ben Reed's place, every fence post where it belongs. You're doing fine work, Rose Lee, fine work."

One day he brought me a little folding stool, the wood carefully smoothed and finished, with a piece of sacking stretched across the frame. "Like the one the white teacher had," he explained, setting it up for me under Mr. Lipscomb's live oak.

The next day I began to work on Grandfather Jim's house, which I had been putting off. It was late summer and the Garden of Eden wasn't as beautiful as it was in the spring, but I included a picture of the white lilac in bloom, as I remembered it. The scent of honeysuckle wrapped itself around me and clung to my skin even after I had gone.

About eleven in the forenoon Nancy Lee or Lora Lee would come to tell me it was time to stop. I would put away my pencils and sketchbook and hurry off to work at Mrs. Bell's.

By late August when I should have been getting ready to go back to school, if there had *been* a school, I had finished a good many of the houses. More people had made up their minds to leave, going back to wherever their families had come from. Mr. Taylor, who really was a tailor, decided to move down to Abilene to open a business there.

Mr. Taylor told Poppa, "I won't stay in a place that doesn't want me as much as Dillon doesn't want me. I have a cousin out there, and he says they treat you fair enough in that town, and that's where we're going. And I swear this to you: I am never coming back here. Not ever."

Turned out a good many folks were feeling that way. It seemed there would not be many of us left, as one family after another announced their intention of moving on and began to pack.

There were fifty-two houses in Freedom-town, in addition to the tailor shop and shoe-maker and mortuary and grocery and café with the Masonic Lodge on the second floor, plus the churches and the Knights of Pythias Hall and what I could remember of the school. I put a house on each page, except the smaller houses, which I grouped together, but at first I spoiled a few pages and had to throw them away. It looked as though the sketchbook would not be large enough for all of Freedom, and Poppa promised to buy me another book. But when he asked the art teachers at the Academy where he could buy a sketchbook, they looked at him like he was crazy and then told him they were sorry, but they couldn't sell him one because his daughter was not enrolled there. So I began to double up.

About this time Mr. Prince, the principal of our school, came by to visit. He brought with him a photograph of last year's graduating class posed in front of Booker T. "It's the only one I have of the school, Rose Lee," he explained, "for all the others burned with the schoolhouse. I'm giving it to you in the event that it would help you to draw a picture of the school from memory."

The photograph didn't show much, just the front door and a part of the window on each side, but it was a beginning. I thought I could remember how it was.

"I don't know just when we're going to start school again, Mrs. Jefferson," he said, turning to Momma who was arranging a stack of clean linens in a wash basket. "We'll be meeting in the Knights of Pythias Hall until we can build a new school. Of course," he added, "I don't know when we'll have a new school. Or where. My immediate problem is, I don't have any teachers. Miss Simpson quit right after the school burned down, and Miss Mitchell handed in her resignation last week. I can't teach all the classes myself."

Aunt Susannah was washing up the breakfast dishes at the kitchen sink. She turned around, soapsuds all the way up to her elbows, and asked, "Are you accepting applications for the position?"

"Why, yes, ma'am, I am," Mr. Prince replied. He had a stiff, formal manner about him that used to make Bessie and Lou Ann and me giggle. "Prince Prince," we called him, behind his back.

"Then please consider my application. I think you'll find me well qualified in grammar, literature, history, and geography. Also mathematics, in a pinch." She smiled. "Science, too, if you're desperate."

Momma and Mr. Prince and I all stared at her. "You want to teach here, Susannah?" Momma asked. "You're not going home?"

My aunt wiped her hands on a dish towel. "I've been thinking about it, and the truth is I feel more at home here than I do in St. Louis," she said. "With so many people deciding to leave, I've decided to come here to stay."

Mr. Prince adjusted his necktie. "In that case," he said, making a little bow to my aunt, "school will begin next week, Miss Jones." He bowed to my momma, who looked like she had just seen a two-headed chicken. "You, too, Rose Lee."

I saw Momma collect herself and get ready to say how nice that was, but I cut in. "I'll only be able to go part time this year," I said. "I got too much to do. I'm still working at Mrs. Bell's as the serving girl, and I need to help Momma with the packing. But mostly I have to make my record of Freedom." It was clear to me my job as an artist was as important as going to school.

"We'll be there, Mr. Prince," Aunt Susannah said firmly, just like I hadn't even opened my mouth. "You may count on us." She turned to Momma. "I'll be going to St. Louis to collect my things," she said, "and then I'll be back."

Momma said, "That'll be fine, Susannah. We'll help however we can."

Mr. Prince was still sitting there, drinking the glass of lemonade she fixed him and, I thought, admiring my aunt Susannah, when Aunt Tillie blustered in the door. She yanked a chair back from the kitchen table, heaved herself into it with a thump, and commenced sobbing, and not quietly, either.

"What on earth, Tillie?" Momma asked. "Is it Cora? Is it the baby?" We knew the baby was due very soon.

"It's that damn Raymond!" Aunt Tillie shouted.

Momma tried her best to calm Aunt Tillie,

but Aunt Tillie wasn't about to be calmed. Mr. Prince looked like he wished he was anywhere but in this kitchen with this wailing woman.

"Lester and him, they drove Edwin Morgan's hearse up to Topeka," she explained finally. "They come back by train a week ago. And they announced they're fixing to move up there, clear to Kansas. They said they got jobs up there, and Edwin Morgan's promised to help them get settled. I want to kick him!" she howled.

"Tillie," Momma said soothingly, "I know how bad you feel about them leaving, the baby coming and all, but I guess Raymond thinks he has a better chance there than he does here."

Aunt Tillie commenced sobbing again, and I understood then that our family was not all going to stay in Dillon. I had counted on us being together, and now even that wasn't going to happen.

LABOR DAY came, an occasion to honor our working men. The Bell family traveled in their car to Fort Worth for the weekend, and Aunt Tillie and I had the day off. But no one was in any mood to celebrate. Thinking we were in need of some cheering up, Pastor Mobley suggested that we carry our picnics out to The Flats and hold a prayer meeting to dedicate the place that had been decided was to be our new home. He got Reverend Delbert from AME to agree. Reluctantly we said we'd go—everybody except Henry. I'm not sure anybody even told Henry we were going, because we all knew he'd make some wild speech about his hero, Marcus Garvey, and how we ought to go to Liberia or some such. Mostly these days we just left Henry alone.

Momma's heart was not in this. No fried chicken, she decided—we would just take a few sandwiches and a bottle of lemonade. But at the last minute she weakened and baked us a peach cobbler.

People got out to The Flats however they could. Our family crowded into Grandfather Jim's wagon. Uncle Walter carried some of the older folks in his taxi along with my cousin Cora, who looked like her baby was coming any day. Most others walked, but it was not a joyful procession. Aunt Susannah wasn't there—she had taken the train up to St. Louis to get her things. I missed her being with us, all dressed up in her red dress and shoes and her red parasol.

It turned out to be the worst idea ever. Instead of the cool shade of our grove by the church, there was not a tree in sight worth mentioning. We gathered in the hot sun, beating away the flies that buzzed around our heads and the chiggers that bit our legs. The preachers made their prayers short, asking God's blessing on our future home. As the prayer meeting ended, the wind shifted, sweeping in the stink of Dillon's open cesspool nearby.

"Phew!" Georgie Ellis, standing near me, said out loud. "If that's the blessing, I don't want *none* of it!"

Georgie's momma on one side and his aunt on the other yanked him by the arms and shushed him. However, those who heard started laughing and it turned out to be one of the better things that happened that day.

Trying to make the best of it, some of the families went to find the plots they had agreed to buy, and Poppa and a couple of the men discussed their prospects for opening businesses out here.

"People always going to need to get their hair cut," Poppa said, and I hoped he was right.

The ladies went ahead and spread their blankets on the rough pasture stubble, but the flies were so mean no one wanted to uncover their picnic food. Silently we packed up and went home again, too miserable to speak. Aunt Tillie didn't even suggest singing.

SEVENTEEN

Moving

THE DAY after Labor Day, which should have been the first day of school, the City of Dillon announced they would build us a new school. But they didn't say exactly where. "If they put it down near Dogtown," I told Momma, "I'm not going. I don't want to graduate that bad."

This was not quite the truth, because I *did* want to graduate. I had thoughts of becoming a teacher, like Aunt Susannah, but so far I hadn't told anybody about those ideas. Still, the notion of going to school anywhere near Dogtown was too much for me.

Then Aunt Susannah came back, and while we waited to find out what was going to happen, she and Mr. Prince did the best they could for us children. Every morning they gathered all twelve grades in the Knights of Pythias Hall and talked to us. That was about all they could do. Our books had burned up in the fire. We had no map, no blackboard, no chalk, not even a tablet and pencil.

"The city has promised us books," Mr. Prince said. "They have some old ones stored away someplace they'll let us have. I don't know just when that will be."

Meantime, all they had to teach us with was what they carried around inside their heads, which proved to be a lot. And Mr. Prince brought his own books from home. Sometimes he talked to us about famous Negroes we should be proud of. Of course we all knew about Booker T. Washington who founded a school in Alabama for colored people, because our old school was named for him. And Mr. Prince liked to talk about Frederick Douglass, who was born a slave and grew up to be an abolitionist — like Miss Firth's people, I thought. He had died a long time ago, in 1895.

But Mr. Prince wanted us to know about some famous *living* Negroes, too, like W. E. B.

Du Bois, who founded the National Association for the Advancement of Colored People.

"When we build our new schoolhouse," the principal said, "we're not going to name it after Mr. Washington. I don't agree with Mr. Washington's ideas that everything coming to the Negro should be *gradual*. I propose that we name the school the W. E. B. Du Bois School."

I raised my hand. "What about Mr. Garvey?" I asked, thinking about my brother's speeches.

"Marcus Garvey is either a charlatan or a genius," Mr. Prince said in measured tones, "and I'm not certain which. A charlatan is a fake. Your brother has shown me copies of Mr. Garvey's publication, *Negro World*. Much that he has to say is sound. If we had our map, I would show you where Liberia is located on the continent of Africa. But in any case, Rose Lee, I don't believe it's appropriate at this time to name our school for him."

At least, I thought, he didn't laugh at me for asking. Then I had another question. "When we going to get that school, Mr. Prince?"

"In time enough for you to graduate, Rose Lee," he said. "That's all I can promise you."

Then Aunt Susannah broke in. "Let's memorize some poetry," she said. "It's good exercise for the mind." And she set about teaching us "The Rime of the Ancient Mariner," a very long poem about a crazy old sailor who shows up at a wedding. She made it very dramatic:

> *The ice was here, the ice was there,*
> *The ice was all around:*
> *It cracked and growled, and roared and howled,*
> *Like noises in a swound!"*

Nobody knew what a *swound* was, but we all got carried away by that poem and tried our best to commit it to memory.

As soon as we were dismissed, I ran home. Momma and Poppa were starting to pack, and every spare minute I had I was to help. I never thought we owned much until it came time to get it ready to move.

SUNDAY was the Lord's Day and supposedly a day of rest, but not for the colored folks of Freedom, not in the fall of 1921. There was too much to be done.

Soon as church service was over, Poppa and Uncle Theo went out to The Flats to clear our patch of ground and mark where our house was to go. They cut logs and sawed them into posts that were sunk into the ground for the house to rest upon. Then they helped with the posts for Grandfather's house, though Grandfather kept insisting he didn't need any help.

The City of Dillon marked out streets running through The Flats, and those who had made up their minds to move out there began naming them for the people who had decided to go someplace else. The main street was Ragsdale Avenue for the doctor, and there was Morgan Street for Bessie's people and Webster Street for the owner of the Sun-Up Café. And then someone suggested naming one Williams, after Grandfather Jim, even though he wasn't going somewhere else, because he was one of the oldest residents of Freedom. So we would be living on Williams Street.

Mr. Alexander, the foreman of the brickyard who always seemed to go along with what Mayor Dixon and the city council wanted, had already moved. It was the first house to go, and he was busy adding an extra room built out of solid brick. "His reward for being so agreeable," Poppa grumbled, watching the brick walls rise.

A plot of ground was set aside for each building to be taken to The Flats, but it was decided that Forgiveness Baptist Church was too hard to move and should be left behind and replaced with a new building. Pastor Mobley asked to store the big bell at Grandfather's house until they got around to building the new church. Grandfather said it was an honor.

The Knights of Pythias Hall was going, but to a separate location, on down Ragsdale Avenue where it turned into Route 16 near Dogtown. There would be no Sun-Up Café, and no one to move Mr. Webster's old building. Same for the doctor's pretty house. The Ragsdales planned to go off and leave it behind for the City of Dillon to knock down or do whatever they wanted to with it.

Then Mr. Lipscomb decided that he was an old man and didn't feel like running a boardinghouse anymore, if he couldn't move it to Buttermilk Hill he wasn't going to move it anyplace, and if the town of Dillon wanted to knock it down, too, they could go ahead and do it. But Mrs. Lipscomb told Grandmother Lila, who passed it on to Momma, that her husband felt so bad about that he would eat hardly anything, and she was worried about him.

That's when Aunt Susannah stunned everybody with another announcement. She had brought over a nice piece of ham, and Momma cooked it up with greens and made some candied yams to go with it for our Sunday supper — Momma had about given up on Aunt Susannah's cooking. "I've bought Dr. Ragsdale's house," my aunt said when we sat down to eat.

Naturally everybody just stared at her. "Dr. Ragsdale's house?" Poppa echoed, sounding disbelieving. "You bought that house, Sue?"

"Yessir, I did. Remember that ring I came here with? The emerald with the little diamonds? Well, I sold it when I went up to St. Louis to arrange for my things. Got enough for it to put a payment down on that house."

I glanced real quick at her finger, and sure enough, the beautiful ring was gone. I couldn't believe I hadn't noticed before.

"Guess the next thing we need to do then," Poppa said, talking slow, "is get it out to The Flats."

ONE BY ONE our houses were hauled away to The Flats. It was a sight nearly everybody turned out to watch. Most of the able-bodied men of Freedom gathered to help. This took place at night when the roads around Dillon were empty of traffic, and those who weren't taking their spell of helping held torches to light the way for those who were.

First they jacked up the house and set wooden runners under it. Then they shoved logs under the runners and hitched the runners to a team of mules, hired from a farmer out near Grover Point and paid for by the city, like they promised. The mule driver clucked his tongue and the mules leaned against the weight of their burden until slowly the house began to roll on the logs. Quickly the men rushed around to the back, grabbed the last log as the runners passed over it, and scrambled to lay that log in front. They did this over and over again as the house inched slowly toward its new site.

The night it was time for our house to go, Momma sent my little sisters and me to stay with Grandmother Lila. Nancy Lee and Lora Lee fell asleep right away in Grandmother's big bed, but I knew there would be no sleep for me that night.

I tried to sketch the scene as our house crept slowly down Logan Street past Grandmother's parlor window, but my figures of men and mules held little resemblance to the real thing. I was about to give up trying when Grandmother Lila laid aside the album quilt she was piecing for Dr. Ragsdale's family, a Bible verse stitched on each square by one of his patients. She peered through her glasses at my drawing of the scene.

"Oh, don't look," I begged. "I can't do people or animals."

"You do them good enough to help us remember," she said, so I kept on with it until I got too tired.

That was the last drawing I would do of Freedom.

The next day I stayed home from school to help Momma unpack, trying to put everything back exactly the way it was. That night I climbed into bed next to my sisters and fell asleep, all worn out. I hung Miss Firth's drawing of Grandfather and me in Mrs. Bell's garden on a nail above my bed. Same bed, same house, but everything different.

My cousin Cora picked the night Aunt Tillie's house was to be moved to have her baby. It was a little boy that Grandmother, who was there for the birthing, said looked exactly like Raymond. They decided to name him Freedom, for the home he was leaving. And the next day Aunt Flora's daughter Grace announced that she and Lester had run off and got married and she was going with him to Topeka. So there was Aunt Flora in our kitchen, bawling just like Aunt Tillie did, and all of us weeping, too.

I had one more blow coming:

"Lewis Hembry's going," Poppa said. "They're moving on up to Oklahoma."

"But they can't!" I cried. First Bessie, and now Lou Ann, my two best friends.

"Can and will, baby," Poppa said. "Asked the railroad for a transfer, and they said they'll give it to him."

If we weren't busy moving houses, we were saying good-bye.

THAT SAME WEEK the Ragsdales left, taking the album quilt Grandmother stitched together for them, and their house was moved out to The Flats and set down across the street from ours. Aunt Susannah set to work fixing it up. People who left gave her the furniture they didn't need or want to take along, and it got so you could go in her house and find a little bit of your old friends and neighbors. Aunt Susannah was about the only person there who seemed to be happy about something.

Finally it was Grandfather's turn to haul his house. It was about the only one left. But Grandmother was still insisting she wasn't going.

"We'll have to do the packing for her," Momma said wearily. "She's being as stubborn as I've ever seen her."

When the men came to move the house, Grandmother Lila refused to come out. "I'm traveling with my house," she said, and she sat down in her rocking chair in the parlor and took out her fancywork.

Momma tried to coax her out, so did Aunt Tillie and Aunt Vinnie and Aunt Flora, but it was no good. She wouldn't budge. Then Grandfather said, "Rose Lee, you go in and sit with her. If she won't come out, we'll just take the house with her in it, that's all."

And so I did as I was told, gladly, and sat in the company rocking chair in Grandmother's parlor while the house she had lived in all her married life moved slowly, slowly through the dark night. It was an odd thing to be inside looking out as the men hollered to each other, bringing the hindmost log up to the front, over and over and over again as we rolled toward The Flats.

"Grandmother," I said, to pass the time while Freedomtown was left behind, "tell me about when you met Grandfather." I was thinking of my trip with him from the fairgrounds on the Fourth of July, and Grandfather's story of his vision of a wife. I wondered if she knew about that.

Grandmother bit off a length of embroidery floss, threaded her needle, and plunged it through the cloth stretched tight on her hoop. "I had a number of young men calling on me," she said. The needle appeared from under the hoop and disappeared again. "Some were handsomer than Jim Williams, some earned plenty more money, but—" Her voice trailed off, and I saw she was smiling.

"But *what?*"

"He was just so *insistent,*" she said. "He kept saying 'I had a vision of you, Lila,' or some such foolishness, and somehow I believed him." She laughed to herself. "Next thing I knew, I was married."

"But how did you know he was the best one, Grandmother? Did you have a dream or anything?"

"No, but I had a feeling. Just a feeling he would be kind. And I was right. Believe it or not, the only thing we ever argued about is this business." She waved her hand to include the house, the men and mules outside, our slow progress toward The Flats.

By the time the sun came up, Grandfather's house stood solidly in its new place. Grandmother rose calmly from her rocking chair, tucked her wiry gray hair into its bun, and marched into her kitchen just like it was any ordinary morning. She built a fire in her cookstove, found her iron skillet, and began frying up some bacon. She put the coffee on to boil and set a pan of biscuits on the stove to heat up.

When breakfast was ready, she called to Grandfather Jim. We sat down at the table, already covered with a snow white cloth embroidered with yellow daisies, and bowed our heads and gave thanks for the bounties that God had bestowed upon us.

Then I went off to school at the Knights of Pythias Hall, taking the long walk down Ragsdale Avenue. The City of Dillon had finally sent over a box of books. We shared them, three to a book.

I had another surprise coming. The next day Mrs. Bell told me she had finally found someone to take my place. Mr. Alexander's brother had moved his family to Dillon, she said, and the girl had experience serving. The new people didn't settle in The Flats. We heard a couple of families were allowed to live out by the flour mill. I was relieved not to have to serve anymore, to tell the truth, although I would miss seeing Catherine Jane from time to time. Just as I expected, she was taking driving lessons from one of her brother's friends, and I sometimes saw her practicing backing Edward's new Model T in and out of the porte cochere.

"Look at this, Rose Lee!" she called. "I'll

take you for a spin one of these days!"

I just smiled and waved.

"You lucky, honey," Aunt Tillie said when I told her I wasn't serving anymore. "I'd just as soon walk out of Mrs. Bell's kitchen and never look back."

But everybody had to keep on working at something, and it was hard. It didn't take Momma long to find out exactly how hard it was going to be to keep doing wash for Dillon ladies now that we lived all the way out in The Flats. How was she going to get the dirty clothes out and the clean clothes back?

"I don't know yet, Rose Lee," Momma admitted. "But I do believe the Lord will take care of us."

I surely did hope so. But so far, it seemed to me, He wasn't doing such a good job. Naturally I didn't say that to Momma. It would have made her mad, even if she secretly agreed with me.

Then she got the notion of hiring Uncle Walter to go around in his taxicab to pick up and deliver, and my new job was to ride with him and go up to the back door of each house while he waited in the taxi.

Poppa had a harder time making do. Only about a third of the families in Freedom had moved to The Flats. The rest had gone away, some clear out of Texas altogether and the others to different places around Dillon, wherever somebody was willing to sell or rent to one or two Negroes, but no more than that. A few people even ended up in Dogtown after all. But the men who still lived in Dillon stopped coming around to the barbershop as often as they once did.

Hour after hour Poppa sat dejectedly in his mostly empty shop, waiting for customers who didn't come. It made me so sad to see him. Then one day he put a CLOSED sign in the window and told Henry he could move his cot into that room, that it wouldn't be used for a barbershop anymore. I wondered where he'd go to look for work.

The Flats generally looked naked and ugly. Nevertheless, Grandfather dug flower beds all around his house and with Jojo and his wagon carted the bricks from his old garden in Freedom to pave the winding paths he laid out in his new Garden of Eden. He found the exact place to plant his white lilac and built a little white picket fence around it. Every time he and Jojo made a trip back to the ruin that had been Freedomtown, he dug up a sapling or two from the banks of the creek or a couple of bushes and hauled them out to The Flats to improve the place. I helped him plant them here and there, although this appeared to me to be a hopeless task. Grandfather didn't see it that way.

"You wait, Rose Lee," he said. "Next spring it's all going to bloom just as pretty as can be. You'll see."

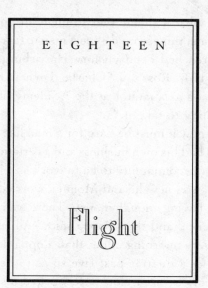

EIGHTEEN

Flight

Mᴏᴍᴍᴀ ʜᴀᴅ ɢᴏɴᴇ to a meeting of the Household of Ruth, what few Ruths there were left to meet, and I was at the kitchen table memorizing the forty-eight states and their capitals when Mr. Ross, the head janitor at the Academy, came by to visit Poppa. Poppa nodded to me, a sign I was to go to my room and leave them to talk. I left the door ajar so I could hear what was said and felt no shame doing that.

First they spoke about this and that, how hard it was being out here in The Flats, where the Masons might hold their lodge meetings now that Mr. Webster's Sun-Up Café was no more, what a shame that so many of our folks had gone, things you'd expect men to talk about. I had reached Pennsylvania, Harrisburg, when I heard Mr. Ross say, "Charlie, I'm here to offer you a job as a janitor at the Academy, if you'd be willing to take it."

I knew it must be hard for a man like Poppa who'd had his own business and a certain standing in the community to go to work as a janitor. But I also knew he and Momma worried about us not having enough money. There was a painful silence, and then Poppa said, "All right."

Every morning after that Poppa left our house at a quarter past five so as to be at the Academy by six o'clock. He worked inside the buildings, cleaning and repairing and whatever else he was given to do, until the girls arrived for their classes at nine. Then Mr. Ross sent all the colored men outside to work. Poppa and the other janitors left their dinner buckets in the maintenance shed. Around noon they were allowed to stop work for an hour and went to the shed to eat and rest and talk.

After the girls left at four o'clock, the men went back to finish their inside work until six. This arrangement was to make sure the Negroes were nowhere around when the white girls were in the classrooms. I guessed this was by order of Dr. Wesley Thompson, who no doubt thought the colored janitors could be a menace to the safety and welfare of the young lady students.

When Poppa came home at seven, Momma had a good supper ready for him. Now that he wasn't keeping the barbershop open until late every evening, we all had supper together. Usually Poppa ate without saying much. For the most part so did Henry, when he was there.

Henry seemed to have changed, to have gone deeper into himself. There were times we didn't see him for days on end. I wondered if the tar-and-feathering had done something to him he might never get over. That, and his disappointment that Poppa and the other men hadn't fought to keep Freedom the way he thought they should, or else made up their minds to pack up and go to Africa with Mr. Garvey. We hadn't heard much about that lately and I wondered if he still planned to go. I couldn't believe he'd actually do it but you never knew with Henry. One thing I did know, though — Henry hated working in the Bells' garden.

Then one night Poppa came home at suppertime with a frown deep as a ditch. "Where's Henry?" he rumbled, washing his hands at the kitchen sink.

Momma was stirring a pot of black-eyed

peas on the stove. "I haven't seen him," she said, and her face tightened with worry. "Why?"

"Rumors going around. I just saw Gus Alexander coming home from the brickyard, and he told me what he heard. I don't like it."

"What kind of rumors?"

"That Henry has been saying things that could get him into a pack of trouble."

Momma pulled out a chair and sat down on the edge of it. "What kind of things?"

"It's not only *what* he's saying but *to who*, according to Gus. In this case, to Edward Bell and Emory Tubbs. Emory's daddy is boss at the brickyard. Mayor Dixon owns it, but Mr. Tubbs runs it even though Gus Alexander would like you to think he's the one in charge. Mr. Tubbs told Gus that Henry was working in Mrs. Bell's garden when Edward came out and told him to stop raking and go wash his new car, and Henry refused. Emory was there and heard it all. Emory told his daddy that Henry not only refused to wash that car but made a speech about why he was refusing, saying how the Negroes are equal to whites even if whites don't treat them that way. And Edward told him to shut up, but Henry just kept on talking and then threw down his rake and walked away."

"Oh, Lord help us," Momma whispered.

"Edward's madder'n a hornet. He's threatening to teach Henry a lesson he won't forget, since he seems to have forgotten the last one so soon."

I sucked in my breath, hearing all this. Poppa had found out that Mr. Tubbs was one of the men who nailed the notices to Mr. Lipscomb's boardinghouse and Mr. Webster's Sun-Up Café as well as Forgiveness Church and Booker T. And I had a pretty good idea it was Emory Tubbs and Edward Bell who were in the bunch that tarred and feathered my brother. I thought of the men in the white robes and hoods, like the one in Mr. Bell's cupboard, who had marched through Freedom and burned a cross by our church.

If they decided Henry was uppity, they'd do something bad, something even worse this time than tar and feathers. They'd horsewhip him for sure. They might even kill him. And they'd be masked so nobody could rightly say who did it. My heart nearly tore a hole clear through my chest when I thought about that.

"What does Gus think we ought to do?" Momma asked in a quavery voice.

"Get Henry out of town, the mood being so ugly now. 'If he was my boy I'd get him out of here, and I'd do it as quick as I could.' That's what he said. Henry can come on home later when this talk blows over and people forget about it."

They were still discussing it, trying to figure out what to do, when Aunt Tillie blustered in and plumped herself down at the table. "My feet hurt," she complained. "Guess you heard the mess your boy's got himself into."

"We haven't talked to Henry yet," Momma said. "What happened?"

"You better ask Henry about *that*. Been shooting his mouth off, mostly. I'd get him as far away from here as can be, if I was you."

That made two people said Henry ought to leave. But where was Henry? Even after all the trouble he had been through, he still didn't stay home in the evenings. And now that he slept in the room that used to be Poppa's barbershop, I had no idea when he was there and when he was not.

THE SHOUTING woke me up. Poppa and Henry were in the kitchen, and they were having a big argument. "Is there any truth to what he said, Henry?" bellowed Poppa, who hardly ever raised his voice, even when I knew he was mad as could be at one of us. "You'd better tell me, boy, because we got to figure out what to do."

Then I heard Momma say, "Oh, please . . . ," so I knew she was there, too.

"Yes, it's true! I told him to wash his own damn car, I'm not his slave. Mr. Lincoln freed the slaves fifty-eight years ago, but Edward Bell hasn't heard the news yet."

"Henry, you're being paid to do what those folks tell you to do. That's the difference. I got to do what Joe Ross tells me to do over at the Academy, and Joe Ross got to do what some white boss tells him to do, but we aren't slaves because we get paid for our work. And anyway, you got no business talking that way to Edward or Emory or anybody else."

"Emory Tubbs turned the hose on me," Henry said sullenly. "I was raking out Mrs. Bell's flower beds by the veranda, and Emory and Edward come out of the house and Emory turns on the garden hose strong and soaks me good, laughing like anything. Then Edward tells me to wash his car, and I say no sir, I won't, and Emory, he keeps playing that stream of water on me, the two of them laughing fit to bust."

Poppa listened. "There's all different kinds of white folks," he said thoughtfully. "Some are kind, long as Negroes stay in their place. Some are mean and would just as soon Negroes all vanish from the face of the earth, except they need somebody to stick around to do their work. And some go way past mean and just hate niggers, no matter what. From what I hear, Mr. Tubbs is a hater. I believe Mr. Tubbs would see you hurt, and hurt bad, with a smile on his face, Henry."

"It's not Tubbs turned the hose on me. It's his son."

"Doesn't matter. You insulted those white boys and now you got to leave, Henry. It's foolish to do otherwise."

"I'm not going, Poppa!"

"It would only be for a little while, Henry." That was Momma's voice, coaxing, wheedling, hoping she'd get what Poppa couldn't by shouting. "You'd be back here in a few weeks, when it's safe again."

"Never going to be safe here, Momma," Henry said. "Not for a black man. Not for *this* black man!"

That's how it went. I lay in bed, curled on my side, not even trying to hear, and wishing I couldn't.

In the end Poppa prevailed. Henry agreed to leave town — "temporarily," they said —

when they convinced him it might bring harm to the rest of us if he didn't.

I thought Momma's heart was going to break. "I'm losing my second son," she said, remembering, I guess, when my brother Jack died.

The plan was this: Henry would not go to Mrs. Bell's that day but was to lie low and get ready to leave on a minute's notice. Poppa would go to the Academy as usual, keeping his ears open for any rumor. Then, if it seemed safe, Grandfather would deliver Henry to the railroad depot in time to catch the night train to Topeka. Maybe Mr. Morgan could help him find work. Raymond and Lester and their wives were already there, so he wouldn't be all alone.

Poppa, looking worn out and downhearted, left way before sunup with only a little sleep to walk to the Academy. "I'll let out the word you're down sick, Henry. And if I sense any trouble, I'll be straight home. Meanwhile, you be ready to travel."

That's when I made up my mind to go over to the Bells' and take Henry's place in the garden for that one day. Maybe I'd hear something. Grandfather might be there, but if he wasn't, it didn't matter. No use telling Momma my part of the plan. I'd just start off as if I was going to visit Grandmother and then head on out Oak Street to Mrs. Bell's.

In the fall of the year Mrs. Bell's garden glowed with rose, lavender, purple, and white asters. White spider lilies popped like miniature fireworks around the stately white house. Clematis blanketed the iron fence with fragrant stars. I thought that even Henry must have come to see the beauty of it, even if he didn't like to work there.

I decided the best thing was to keep myself out of sight behind the garden shed. I set to work cleaning up in the vegetable patch, picking off the last of the ripe tomatoes from the wilting vines. Then I tidied up the shed, making sure all the tools were clean and bright in their proper places. I stayed busy but alert to comings and goings, doors slamming, voices.

Early in the afternoon after lunch had been served inside the big house, I heard Edward's voice and then a second voice that I took to be Emory Tubbs's by the porte cochere. "Where d'you s'pose that no-good nigger is today?" Edward said quite clearly, and then the other voice said something about it being "time to whip some respect into him." That voice went straight through me and made my skin prickle.

I peeped around the corner of the shed and saw Edward and Emory climb into the Model

T, and the two of them drove off, leaving Mr. Bell's Packard car parked under the roof. They'd do it, I thought. And I knew I had to do something in a hurry.

I closed up the shed and strolled in through the kitchen door, calm as you please but it was all an act. Ella, the new serving girl, glanced up nervously from drying the lunch dishes. "Afternoon, Aunt Tillie," I sang out.

"What you doing here?" Aunt Tillie asked.

"Just stopped by to help out," I said, hoping my voice sounded steadier than I felt. "Henry's not feeling good, so I said I'd come by and finish up for him."

"Be feeling a lot worse if he doesn't watch himself."

"Are Catherine Jane and Mrs. Bell around?" I asked, innocent as cream.

"Guess so." She jerked her head to tell me they were upstairs.

I picked up a couple of mixing bowls I knew belonged in the pantry. "Here, Ella, I'll put these away for you," I said. Soon as those bowls were on the shelf and I thought I could manage it, I skinned through the door at the bottom of the backstairs and shut it fast behind me. With both doors closed at top and bottom, the stairwell was dark as night. Quiet as a mouse I crept up the stairs, fingering my way along the wall, and stood listening at the top until I was pretty sure nobody was in the upstairs hall. Then I opened the door a crack and peered out. Quick as lightning I crossed that hall and tapped on Catherine Jane's door.

"Who is it?"

"It's me, Rose Lee," I whispered.

She flung open the door, a big smile spreading on her face, glad to see me. I held my finger up to my lips for silence. "Shhhh," I hissed. "I got to talk to you."

I could see she loved this, a secret visit. I stepped into her room and let her shut the door. "What's going on, Rose Lee?"

"I need your help," I said. "Henry's in trouble."

The smile faded. "I know," she said. "Edward was talking about him last night at dinner. Your brother's a real troublemaker, to hear Edward tell it."

"Maybe. But I fear for him."

"I don't think Edward would do anything . . ." she trailed off, maybe not believing what she was saying.

"Maybe not Edward," I allowed, "but Emory. Emory would."

Catherine Jane considered that, her hand cupping her chin.

"We've got to get him away someplace safe,"

I told her. "He's planning to take the train on up to Kansas, but I'm afraid something bad's going to happen before he has a chance to go."

I was trying to make her see that she had to help me save Henry without coming right out and saying it was *her* brother she was saving *my* brother from.

"When does the train leave?"

"Tonight. But plenty could happen before then. They'll catch him at the depot, or pull him off the train. He needs to get far enough away from here that they won't bother to go after him." I took a deep breath and raced ahead. "I have an idea that you could drive him someplace safe. It wouldn't be too far. Just up to Blue Springs, to our cousin's farm. He'd be safe hidden in your car, with a white girl driving. No-body'd bother you." Then I waited, jumpy as a flea, to see what she'd say. If I was lucky, she'd do it. If I wasn't, she'd run and tell her momma and I'd be in the most trouble I've been in in my whole life.

"All right, Rose Lee," she said, hardly even stopping to think about it. "What are you wait-ing for? Let's go."

"You mean it? You'll drive Henry?"

"Yes. I've been thinking a lot, and I think my whole family and all their friends are wrong about what they did to your people. Miss Firth helped me to see that. I argue with my parents about it all the time, but of course they don't take me seriously. Well, this is my chance to show them I can stand up for what I believe, just like Miss Firth did."

"You could get into a good bit of trouble." I felt I had to warn her, just not scare her off.

"I *know* that! Come on. Mother's lying down with a headache, and Daddy walked over to his office to get some papers. If we're going to do it, we better go now, before she wakes up or he comes back, and before Edward and Emory have a chance to get their friends together for whatever they're planning."

"Don't you think you should leave a note? Your momma's likely to think you've been kidnapped."

"Good idea." She scribbled something on a slip of paper and propped it on her dressing table. "ON AN ERRAND OF MERCY," it said. "BACK SOON. LOVE, CJ."

Down the front staircase we flew, through the east parlor and out the side door with the etched glass to where the big Packard waited beside the house. Catherine Jane got it started with hardly any trouble, and in no time at all we were on our way down Oak Street.

"This is the first time I've driven this car,"

she said as I directed her to The Flats. "I've only ever driven Edward's."

I was glad she hadn't told me that before. I'd have been even more scared.

"My," she said, driving up Williams Street, "I certainly understand why you wanted to stay in your old place. There are hardly any trees here at all."

It being Saturday, Poppa came home from the Academy at noon. He had agreed to open his barbershop that one afternoon a week, to take care of Pastor Mobley, Mr. Lipscomb, Mr. Prince, and a few of the other regular customers who were still around. When Catherine Jane parked her father's Packard by our veranda, several startled faces appeared at the window. I got out and waved, so they'd know it was nothing to be afraid of.

"This is Catherine Jane Bell. We've come for Henry," I announced. "I heard Emory Tubbs talking" — I stated it that way, without mentioning Edward, to spare Catherine Jane's feelings — "and I think they're planning to do something soon. I heard them say something about 'time to whip some respect into him.' Catherine Jane has kindly offered to drive Henry up to Blue Springs, to Cousin Jake's. Jake can take him on up to Gainesville to get the train tomorrow or the next day. I'm going with them so Catherine Jane doesn't have to drive all the way back by herself."

"No," Momma said without giving it even one second of consideration.

"We surely do thank you, Miss Catherine Jane," Poppa said gently, "but it could be dangerous. For both of you."

"It's my duty," Catherine Jane responded. I thought she sounded brave. Her lessons with Miss Firth had done her some good, even if she wasn't talented in art.

"Nobody's going to stop a white girl," I argued. "We'll hide Henry in the backseat until we're well away from here."

"No!"

This was not unexpected. There then followed a whole lot of debate and confusion, about whether this was the right thing to do. While they were arguing, I took Catherine Jane inside and went to find Henry.

Henry was ready, some clean clothes rolled in a blanket and his dinner bucket with sandwiches Momma fixed for him, as though he was going off to work. I told him Catherine Jane was waiting in the barbershop. I thought he was going to jump right through the window.

"I'm not traveling anywhere with any white girl!" Henry roared. "And Edward Bell's sister in the bargain! Have you gone crazy, Rose Lee? You know what they'd do to me if they ever caught me in the same car with her?"

I knew, everybody knew, that any Negro man caught around a white woman could be hung. "Not going to catch you, Henry," I said. "Unless you stand around here all day fussing about it."

We might be standing there yet, still fussing about it, if Mr. Gus Alexander hadn't come running up, out of breath, and told us Mr. Tubbs himself had hinted that his boy Emory and some others were forming up right then to come and fetch Henry for that respect he was to be taught. "If that boy's got the brains you tell me he does," Mr. Alexander said, "he'll go while the going's good."

Then Mr. Alexander noticed the Packard automobile parked in front of our house and squinted at it. "Whose is that?"

"I'm thinking of buying it, Gus," Mr. Lipscomb said, smooth as butter. Nobody entirely trusted Mr. Alexander, who always seemed to lean toward the white folks' side of things.

And then Pastor Mobley hooked Mr. Alexander by the elbow and began to edge him away, up Williams Street toward his house with the new brick room, saying, "There's something I've been wanting to discuss with you, Gus."

We all knew that the less Mr. Alexander found out about this the better.

It was Catherine Jane who finally swayed Momma and Poppa, convincing them she could safely take Henry wherever he needed to go. But they were still insisting I wasn't the one to go with her.

At that moment Aunt Susannah came across the street to see what was going on. She had taken to wearing faded housedresses and a do-rag like the other colored ladies wore and wasn't half as stylish as she was when she first came. I was sorry Catherine Jane hadn't seen her like that. Aunt Susannah walked right up to Catherine Jane and introduced herself and announced that she was going to Blue Springs, and that was that. I tried pointing out that she had never been to Cousin Jake's and didn't know the way, but Aunt Susannah said, "Don't forget I teach geography, Rose Lee. I'll find it." I swallowed my disappointment.

Henry was plenty angry and disgusted that he was being saved by a white girl and his own aunt, but nevertheless he set his bundle and his dinner bucket in the backseat of the Packard. While Aunt Susannah went home for her purse and everybody was still giving him advice, I ran into the house and got my sketchbook from its hiding place under our mattress.

Everything was in that book—all the houses, all buildings that had been so important to us, our whole world. I had included a little map of the neighborhood, too, showing the streets and the location of each house. Aunt Susannah helped me do that one evening. She was surprised, I think, at how well I managed to get it all down.

I thumbed through the book in a hurry until I came to the drawing of our house. I intended to tear out that one sketch and give it to Henry as a keepsake. But something made me change my mind.

I shut the sketchbook and put it in Henry's hands. "Take this with you," I said. "So you'll remember to come back."

Henry studied it, turning the pages. He hadn't seen it before. "You did this?"

"I've been working on it since I found out we had to leave Freedom," I told him proudly. "So we'd have a record."

"But this is your book, Rose Lee. I can't take it."

"Yes, you can. I want you to. I can make a new one," I insisted, and at that moment I thought I could remember everything.

"All right," Henry said. "Now write something on it."

I took it from him and wrote, "A memory

of Freedomtown from your loving sister, Rose Lee Jefferson, October 1921."

Then Henry did something unexpected, because we weren't close like that: he took a step toward me and hugged me, once, quick, and stepped back. "I promise to take care of your book and bring it home safe," he said and climbed into the backseat. "You be good now."

When he was settled down with one of Momma's counterpanes spread over him, you couldn't tell if you were driving by that anyone was back there. Aunt Susannah crossed the street, all dressed up in her flame red dress and her red shoes and red hat and settled herself in the passenger seat. Catherine Jane slid behind the wheel, waved once, her pale fingers fluttering out the window, and drove off. We watched them go, not knowing when we'd see my brother again.

NINETEEN

Lilacs

FALL PASSED and winter came, dragging by slow as a house moved by mules. It rained day after day, and The Flats flooded, worse than it ever did in Freedom. Grandfather was out day after day, and sometimes far into the night, building dirt levees around his garden to keep the water out. Momma pleaded with him not to work so hard, and Grandmother scolded him.

"You have no business out there, Jim Williams! An old man like you!"

"Just trying to make you a pretty garden, Lila," he called back and went on doing what he wanted. I noticed that he was getting slow about it, moving stiffly, and sometimes he complained about his joints hurting him.

Late in the winter he went back to work at Mrs. Bell's, cleaning up her yard, hauling away broken branches, gathering wet leaves. With Henry gone, Grandfather postponed retirement. I went to help sometimes late in the afternoon.

In early March, the mayor of Dillon finally announced that a new colored school would be erected halfway between The Flats and Dogtown. The men of Forgiveness Baptist discussed plans to build a new church, but it would take a while to raise the money.

All winter long Momma managed to keep her washing business alive, with assistance from Uncle Walter and me. I was still in charge of the pickup and delivery, but I took my younger sisters along to learn. They were getting bigger now, too, and wanting to help. Then one day Poppa quit his job at the Academy, and he and Mr. Lipscomb went together on a business venture, opening a small general store. It wasn't much of a success right from the beginning, and Poppa began to talk of looking for work with the railroad.

I rarely saw Catherine Jane. She was forbidden to speak to me after the day she drove

Henry up to Blue Springs. When she got home late that evening — they'd had a flat tire or some kind of car trouble on the way back — her parents were beside themselves with worry and anger. Despite all their threats, Catherine Jane refused to tell them where she had gone or why, but Ella, the new serving maid, told them she'd seen Catherine Jane driving off with me.

The night of Henry's flight, word had gone out that we were all to stay in our houses, ready for trouble. Around ten o'clock, not long after Aunt Susannah got back, walking all the way out from the courthouse where Catherine Jane dropped her off, a couple of cars full of young white men drove slowly through The Flats without stopping. I recognized Edward's Model T. "We'll get you, nigger!" someone yelled. They came back the next two nights, but then it stopped. They must have gotten tired of it.

Spring came whether we were ready for it or not. Purple grape hyacinths bloomed along the fence, and blue and white pansies turned up their little faces beside the brick walks. Stately white irises flowered by the house. I spent hours pulling up dandelions that sprang up everywhere you looked.

I began a new book of drawings to take the place of the one I gave Henry. I figured the plain old tablets I used in the beginning were good enough, but I guess I had gotten spoiled — those blue lines bothered me. It surprised me how fast the memories faded, little things like the posts on a veranda.

Although I had been avoiding it, I finally made myself go back to the place where Freedomtown had been. Of course I ended up weeping bitter tears. I could walk up Logan Street and tell exactly where our house had been — the posts, the half-buried logs, were still in place. A few of the old houses were still there, not yet torn down but already looking sadly neglected. There were the remnants of Grandfather's former Garden of Eden, the way the first one must have looked when Adam and Eve were driven out after the Fall, bleak and deserted. There were the burned-out remains of Booker T., and the shell of Forgiveness Baptist.

Mr. Prince had found a use for the church's rough pews at the Knights of Pythias Hall where a few of us still struggled for an education. When we all knew "The Rime of the Ancient Mariner," Aunt Susannah started us on "The Lady of Shalott," by Alfred, Lord Tennyson, another of those English poets she favored. I never took to it as much as I did the one about the crazy sailor.

Freedomtown had ceased to exist. It was

dead, gone, only a memory. Sadly I turned back to our new home in The Flats. I hated its ugliness.

THREE DAYS before Easter, which came late that year, Grandfather took sick. One day he came home from Mrs. Bell's and climbed into his bed. "I'm tired, Lila, that's all," he explained and fell asleep. The next morning his skin was parched with fever. In another time I would have run for Dr. Ragsdale, but our doctor was long gone. Instead I raced all the way to the white doctor by the courthouse square who was said to take colored patients. But Dr. Fredericks told me I'd have to bring Grandfather into his clinic. He could not be persuaded to come out to The Flats. Grandfather refused to go to the clinic. "Never mind," he said wearily.

All of his family was present when Grandfather Jim Williams departed this life. All, that is, save Henry, who wrote that he didn't like Topeka and planned to head west to Colorado, to look for work as a ranch hand while he tried to save enough money to go to Liberia. We gathered about the bed Grandmother and Grandfather had shared for fifty-two years, seven months, and three days, and we said good-bye to him. It seemed he was sleeping, but then he opened his eyes and looked around from one to the other. His glance fell upon me.

"The white lilac, Rose Lee," he whispered. "Take care of it for me."

"I will," I promised, though I was crying too much to say it plain.

After that it seemed he simply went away. "To a better land and a better life," Pastor Mobley assured us.

Aunt Tillie started to hum. "Deep, deep river, Lord," she sang, and we joined in. "I want to cross over into campground."

We buried Grandfather in the little Negro cemetery on the other side of the river, his grave outlined with seashells, returned to our work, and gradually went on with our lives. Uncle Theo decided he was getting too old to work at the brickyard and took Grandfather's place in Mrs. Bell's garden, but it was never quite the same again. At least, not to me.

Before long there was no trace of Freedom. The last of the houses was knocked down, and soon the town made a park there, with new flower beds and benches and playing fields. They built a bandstand and a ball diamond and a lily pond with a fountain in the middle and all kinds of goldfish. Everyone admired the magnificent old trees. That park became the pride of Dillon.

I kept my promise, best I could, to take care of Grandfather's precious white lilac. Long as I lived in The Flats, that bush survived, even after Grandmother Lila, too, crossed over into campground. When I grew up and moved away, had my own home and family and garden elsewhere in Dillon, I took the white lilac with me, but it didn't bloom much, not like it used to. Finally it just seemed to give up and die, the way Grandfather did.

Years later if you asked anybody what ever happened to Freedomtown, they didn't have the least idea what you were talking about. White folks claimed they never heard of it. Black folks must have decided it was better to forget. But not all of us did.

A Note from the Author

ON FEBRUARY 28, 1991, I attended the dedication of a historic marker in the city park a few blocks from my home in Denton, Texas. A newcomer to Denton, an attractive university town forty miles north of Dallas, I was curious about its history.

This is what I read on the bronze plaque unveiled that blustery day near the pretty stone arch bridge across Pecan Creek:

On this site from the late 19th century until 1922 stood the thriving community of Quakertown. This African-American community was founded in the years following Reconstruction and was named, according to one account, to honor the abolitionist Pennsylvania Quakers. In its heyday, Quakertown contained fiftyeight [*sic*] families, stores, restaurants, a doctor's office, a mortuary and three churches.

In April of 1921, a bond election was held to raise $75,000, to create a city park on the 27 acre Quakertown site. In spite of opposition from the residents, this proposal passed 367 to 240. By 1923, the residents of Quakertown were required to move. Many of these families moved to the Solomon Hill and Hiram additions in East Denton. The former Quakertown residents and their descendants continue to contribute to the community life of Denton.

The next day I began to learn what I could about Quakertown, which had not only disappeared but had been a taboo subject among both blacks and whites for many years until a graduate student at Texas Women's University delved into a historical research project and came up with long-forgotten records.

The reason for the taboo is not hard to imagine. Blacks were afraid — if it happened once, it could happen again. Whites were embarrassed by the heartlessness of an earlier generation.

The lives of African Americans in Texas in the early 1920s were always difficult. The Ku Klux Klan was at its peak with over 100,000 members in the state, and lynchings were not unheard of. Some historians claim that two black men were removed from the Denton jail and flogged during this period. Jim Crow laws condemned African Americans to separate — and invariably inferior — schools, restaurants, railroad cars, movies, and other public facilities. Despite Constitutional amendments granting them the right to vote, blacks were politically powerless. African Americans who dared to speak out on their own behalf — or whites who spoke out for them — were threatened with violence. There seemed to be no way the black families of Denton in 1921 could stop the city from forcing them out of their homes.

The Great Migration of southern Negroes to northern cities that reached its peak in the 1920s was apparently not considered an option by the citizens of Quakertown. My theory is that this is because Denton lies not in the deep South but on the fault line between the South, which includes Dallas, and the West, which begins at Fort Worth. Those who left Denton sought many different destinations, often joining family members in areas as far away as California. Many who stayed behind simply moved across town, away from the thriving community that had been their home, accepting the new location offered by the city. The new neighborhood was a place to live, but it wasn't a community anymore. The heart and soul had gone out of it.

White Lilacs is a novel inspired by what I learned about Quakertown. I wish to acknowledge the following sources: "The Quakertown Story" by Michele Powers Glaze as it appeared in *The Denton Review* (published by the Historical Society of Denton County, Winter 1991) and *Quakertown 1870–1922* edited by Letitia deBurgos (published by the Denton County Historical Commission, 1991). Although Rose Lee Jefferson, her family and friends, the Bell family, Miss Emily Firth, and the citizens of the fictional Freedom are all my creation, many of the events in their story and the story of Freedomtown and Dillon are based on what actually happened here more than seventy years ago.

DENTON, TEXAS
July 1992